The Norths Are Dazzled by the Murderous Power of MIND OVER MATTER!

"Like Conan Doyle's London, the Lockridges' New York has a lasting magic. There are taxis waiting at every corner, special little French restaurants, and perfect martinis. Even murder sparkles with big city sophistication. For everyone who remembers New York in the Forties and for everyone who wishes he did."

—Emma Lathen

"The versatility of Frances and Richard Lockridge knows almost no bounds."

—*New York Times*

"This husband and wife team is unexcelled in the field of mystery writing when it comes to a completely entertaining crime story."

—*St. Louis Post-Dispatch*

Pam and Jerry North made their first appearance in *The New Yorker* in the 1930s. In 1940, Richard Lockridge's first book-length mystery, *The Norths Meet Murder*, was published. Richard and Frances Lockridge went on to write dozens of Mr. and Mrs. North books, as well as numerous other mysteries. The Norths became the stars of a Broadway play and a movie as well as a long-running radio program and popular television

D0206172

Books by Richard and Frances Lockridge

Murder Within Murder #1
Murder Comes First #2
Murder in a Hurry #3
Death Takes a Bow #4
The Judge Is Reversed #5
Voyage Into Violence #6
Murder by the Book #7
Murder Is Served #8
Death of an Angel #9
Murder Has Its Points #10
Murder Is Suggested #11

Published by POCKET BOOKS

MURDER
IS
SUGGESTED

RICHARD AND
FRANCES LOCKRIDGE

PUBLISHED BY POCKET BOOKS NEW YORK

POCKET BOOKS, a division of Simon & Schuster, Inc.
1230 Avenue of the Americas, New York, N.Y. 10020

Published by arrangement with Harper & Row Publishers, Inc.
Library of Congress Catalog Card Number: 59-13947

ISBN: 0-671-47332-8

First Pocket Books printing July, 1984

10 9 8 7 6 5 4 3 2 1

POCKET and colophon are registered trademarks
of Simon & Schuster, Inc.

Printed in the U.S.A.

In Memory of the Cat Named
Martini
1945–1959

MURDER
IS
SUGGESTED

1

Standing at the third-floor window, William Weigand could look north and west and see the Hudson River. He could not, to be sure, see a great deal of it—a narrow slice of river had been Professor Jameson Elwell's share. Such views are rationed in Manhattan, and rationed grudgingly. But there was moonlight on what Weigand could see of the Hudson; a tug, coaxing a string of barges upstream, moved in whiteness against black shadows etched on shining water. Weigand closed his eyes, which were tired, and opened them again to see the river fresh. A moment of tranquillity—

Someone knocked at the door of the room which had, evidently, been Professor Elwell's office and Weigand turned from the window and nodded to Sergeant Mullins, who opened the door. "Mr. Carl Hunter," a policeman who remained invisible told Mullins, and a tall young man in a narrow gray suit—a man in a button-down shirt; a man with close-trimmed hair—came into the room. He stopped just inside the door, which closed behind him and said, "You wanted to see me?" and then, without waiting for an answer, walked across the room to a wide desk.

There was a small, silver clock on the desk. The young man in the gray suit picked the clock up and looked at it. He turned it over in his hands and wound it, and looked at it again. Then he took two long steps away from the desk and threw the clock into the black mouth of a fireplace. It broke noisily. The young man looked at the remains of the clock for a moment, brushed his hands together briskly and turned back to face Captain William Weigand, of Homicide, Manhattan West, and Sergeant Aloysius Mullins.

The young man had a square face and intelligent-looking gray eyes.

He said, "You wanted—?" and then, it was evident, was stopped by what he saw in the faces he looked at. This was understandable; Mullins's mouth was somewhat open. Mullins's blue eyes were filled with consternation.

"Oh," Mr. Carl Hunter said, in the tone of one who has just got the point. "I suppose you want—" With that, before he paused again, he seemed a little irritated. "It kept on losing time," he said. "What's the use of a clock that keeps on losing time?"

Mullins said, "Lookit, mister," in a harsh voice. "What you think you're—"

"All right, Mullins," Weigand said, and Mullins—who is a large man with the appearance of a policeman—said, with reluctance, "O.K., Loot. Only—"

"Do you always break clocks that run slow, Mr. Hunter?" Weigand asked the young man, who looked puzzled for a moment and then shook his head, but

10

shook it uncertainly. The question seemed to have made him uneasy.

"I guess not," he said. "Silly thing to do, wasn't it? Be interesting to trace the psychological motivation if—" He let that trail off. "They tell me," he said, "that a pretty bad thing's happened. That Professor Elwell—"

"Right," Weigand said. "Professor Elwell's dead, Mr. Hunter. Been dead since a little after three this afternoon."

"The man who came around," Hunter said. "Said you wanted to see me—what he said was, 'The captain would like to ask you a couple of things'—he said 'about an accident.' But from the look of things—"

"Right," Weigand said. "Professor Elwell was murdered, Mr. Hunter. It must have been quite soon after you left this afternoon."

"He was fine when I left," Hunter said, quickly. And that was what Weigand had supposed he would say, since it could hardly be expected that, under the circumstances, he would say anything else.

"Right," Weigand said again. "I wonder if you—"

He paused. Mullins had crossed to the fireplace. He looked down at the clock momentarily and then squatted and picked the clock up. He looked at it and then looked at the watch on his thick wrist. He stood up, then.

"Funny thing, Loot-I-mean-captain," Mullins said. "Clock says nine-thirteen. And you know what time it is? Nine-seventeen. So when this character threw it there and it stopped—see what I mean?" He looked at Weigand; then, with a different expression, at the young man in the narrow gray suit. "So what about it, mister?" Mullins said.

"When I looked at it—" Carl Hunter said, but then he seemed momentarily bewildered. "I was sure it was slow," he said. Now uneasiness was in his voice.

It was, Weigand thought, the uneasiness of a puzzled man. Or, of course, of a man who wished to appear puzzled. The investigation could not, Bill Weigand thought, be said to be beginning in a very orderly fashion. It was almost as if—He smiled faintly to himself, although he did not feel particularly like smiling, and had not for several hours. The affair was starting in a "screwy" fashion. But Mr. and Mrs. North were not in it. At least—

He had got into it himself rather later than he would have liked. He had got back to his office in West Twentieth Street at a few minutes after five, intending only a quick look around before calling it a day, and feeling altogether ready to call it a day. He was tired, then, and his throat was dry and his eyes smarted. He had smoked too many cigarettes in courtroom corridors, and been too bored. Home and a cool drink—it was warm for October—and the tranquillity which, at such parched moments, was to be found also in the quiet of greenish eyes and the clarity of—

He was standing at his desk, calling it a day (and good riddance) when the telephone rang. It was not any telephone, ringing for any policeman. Send not to ask, Weigand thought gloomily, and picked the instrument up and said, "Weigand."

"His nibs," the telephone said.

"Put him on," Weigand said and, instinctively, held the receiver at a little distance from his ear.

"Where the hell have *you* been?" Deputy Chief Inspector Artemus O'Malley shouted. Weigand removed the receiver further from his ear. The inspector could put a really nasty emphasis on the word "you." Also, the inspector knew perfectly well where Weigand had been. Such matters are not unrecorded.

"General Sessions," Weigand said. "Summoned as a rebuttal witness in the case of People of the State of New York versus 'Puggy' Wormser. To testify that, no, we didn't beat him with rubber hose."

"Didn't we?" O'Malley asked, momentarily diverted.

"No."

"Kid gloves," O'Malley said. "That's what's the trouble nowadays. G.d. kid gloves."

It was a subject by which Deputy Chief Inspector Artemus O'Malley could easily be diverted. O'Malley was a graduate of the school of hard knocks, which he believed it more blessed to give than to receive. Left to himself he would expatiate indefinitely on the theme.

"You wanted me?" Weigand said, not leaving O'Malley to himself.

To this, Deputy Chief Inspector Artemus O'Malley said, "Huh?" in honest, but momentary, bewilderment. He made up for it. He said, "What did you think I called for, captain?" Weigand withdrew the receiver another half inch from his ear. He said, mildly, that he had just got in. There was no point in saying that he had, also, been just about to go off. It was already evident that he wasn't.

"Some g.d. professor's got himself killed," O'Malley said. (He said "g.d.," circumventing the Holy Name Society.) "Seems like he's got a name." O'Malley disliked murder victims who had names. Names stirred up newspapers. "Sent it through hours ago."

"I was—" Weigand began.

"I know where you were," O'Malley said. "You think I can't hear, Bill? What the hell's the matter with that outfit of yours?"

"Nothing," Weigand said. "If it came through, somebody's on it. Lieutenant Graham—no, he's on the Birdy kill. Mullins, probably."

"Find out," O'Malley said. "Get on it. You young squirts."

"Right," Weigand said.

"Keep in touch," O'Malley said. "I'll be home. Or maybe at Paddy's Grill. That is, if there's something you can't handle. Otherwise—"

"Right," Weigand said.

He hung up, complete with instructions—and, in spite of weariness, of acute realization that policemen may not plan on tranquil evenings, somewhat amused. There was only one O'Malley, and he to be disturbed only if the heavens fell. And a good cop, all the same, and an appreciative one. (Hence Weigand's captaincy, fairly early on, although Bill Weigand could not convincingly argue, even to himself, that he was *too* young a squirt.) Weigand used the telephone again.

Mullins was on it, along with the precinct men and, in the normal course, a detective assigned to the district attorney's Homicide Bureau. Along, also, with lab men, with photographers, with, in a word, everybody.

"It" had begun at precisely eleven minutes after three o'clock on that afternoon of Wednesday, October twenty-second.

It had begun with a sound in the ears of a young woman who had said, with professional cheer, "Operator?"

The voice had been that of a man—a man who spoke

14

with obvious and great effort, as if each articulated sound took more strength than the man had left.

"This is emerg—" the man said, and the voice faded.

"I don't—" the operator began, and the other words came—came faint, came in gasps, so that they were just understandable. *"Doctor,"* the man said. "Been shot. Ambu—"

But there the words stopped.

"I'm sorry, sir," the operator said, automatically. And then said, "Hello? Hel*lo!*" And there was no answer at all.

The line remained open, which helped. An open line from a dial telephone may be tracked down, given time enough. It was tracked down. The call had come from the number listed to Jameson Elwell, who lived on the upper west side of Manhattan, on one of the streets which slope sharply down from West End Avenue toward Riverside Drive.

But the tracing of calls from dial telephones does take time, and the uniformed men of the first squad car found Jameson Elwell dead. He had bled to death from a gunshot wound, in what was clearly his office on the third and top floor of a narrow house. There had indeed been nobody else in the house when the police arrived. It had been necessary to force the door of the house—the heavy door with polished brass knob, two steps below sidewalk level. That had taken time, also, and it had taken more time to find Jameson Elwell, since they had, quite naturally, worked upward through the house.

He was slumped over his desk, his hand still on the telephone, but the hand limp now. The desk blotter was soaked with his blood, and blood had trickled to the floor around the desk. But it would not, the assistant medical examiner said, when he had looked and touched, have made any real difference if they had got there more quickly. With a bullet so near the heart, the remarkable thing was that Jameson Elwell had been able to dial the operator, to say as much as he had said—almost to complete the word "ambulance."

Jameson Elwell—more fully, a quick check revealed, Jameson Elwell, Ph.D., Professor of Psychology, Dyckman University. Author of—author of a row of books, three shelf-feet of books. (*Suggestibility in Children; Technics of Suggestion*. Etcetera and etcetera.)

More fully still—a rather heavy man of a little under normal height; a white-haired man with clipped white mustache; a blue-eyed man. Before so much blood had drained out of him, probably a ruddy man. A man in his middle sixties. (He would, it turned out, have been sixty-five on December twenty-third, if he had lived so long.) A man shot once, from no considerable distance—probably from across the desk only—with what appeared to have been (and was subsequently proved to have been) a .32 calibre revolver. Once, had been quite enough. No revolver was in the room. There was nothing on the desk except the blood-soaked blotter, two pens in a holder, a small silver clock faced so that, had his eyes not been dimmed by death, Professor Elwell might have noted exactly when he died.

It had been five-thirty, or thereabouts, when Bill Weigand dialed a familiar number and heard a familiar voice and said, "Dorian. I—"

He did not need to finish. He could see her. She had answered quickly; would have moved quickly across

16

the room—the room with windows looking out over the East River—moved with the grace of a dancer, almost of a cat. She would be standing now, with the tips of fingers just touching the telephone table, with the telephone held to her ear with the other hand. She would be standing with uncalculated grace, as she moved with grace.

"Oh," Dorian Weigand said into the telephone. The syllable was flat, deflated. "Not again."

But it was again.

"You would marry a policeman," Bill Weigand said. "After all due warning."

"Wouldn't I just," Dorian said. "I suppose you've no idea? But have you ever?"

"No," Bill said. "People will get themselves killed."

"Pam and Jerry are—" Dorian said.

"I know," Bill said. "Drink a round for me. And, darling—"

Bill Weigand felt somewhat better when he replaced the telephone in its cradle—somewhat, but not much. Even a voice, diminished by electric impulses, a little scratched by them, was something. Not sight, not touch—just a little something. Bill Weigand drove his car north from Twentieth Street, up the elevated highway, and off it at Seventy-second and, first, to the precinct station house, where he caught up with things—where he looked at photographs and sketches; where he learned that there were fingerprints (not, so far, on record) on the surface of the desk opposite the dead man; that dust from the room was at the lab; that Professor Elwell had been alone in the house when he died because he had given his houseman, one Delbert Higgins—"Delbert?" Yes, Delbert—the afternoon off.

17

And—that, before he left, Higgins had admitted a man named Carl Hunter who was, Higgins thought, one of the professor's students and was, whatever else, a man who frequently visited the professor, almost always in his office.

Mr. Hunter had arrived at about two o'clock. Higgins had let him in, had heard him say that the professor expected him, had watched him go up the stairs. Higgins had then, himself, gone elsewhere. He had gone to a movie. He had returned to the house and found the police there.

Where Higgins had gone did not, for the moment at least, seem of importance. Mr. Hunter might be; Mr. Hunter had been found (from university records) to live in a one-room apartment off upper Broadway and to be, at present, not in it. He was being waited for.

Nobody had been found who had heard the firing of the bullet which killed Jameson Elwell. Nobody had, as yet, been found who remembered seeing a man—presumably young, if a student—leaving the Elwell house either before or after three o'clock.

The house was Elwell's own. Preliminary enquiries suggested that Elwell had not needed to live on a professor's salary. By the time Weigand reached the precinct house, it was also known that Professor Elwell was a widower of some years' standing; that he had a brother living in Westport, Connecticut—notified; on his way in—a niece and two nephews, one of the latter attending Dyckman and the other in the army; the niece married and living in Scranton, Pennsylvania; that he had had a daughter who, six months before, had been killed in an automobile accident on the Merritt Parkway.

Weigand's hands were, in short, piled high with facts, for some of which he might sometime have use. There was no urgent need to visit the house in which Professor Elwell had died; to look at the dried blood which had drained out of him. Experts had been there, experts would be there again. There were many papers to go through and—

"By the way," Weigand said, "what's this?"

This was a door indicated in a sketch plan of the professor's office.

"Door to a closet," the precinct detective captain told him. "Record files on both sides; file cards. God knows what all. Putting a couple of men on it tomorrow unless you—"

"Thanks," Weigand said. "You go right ahead, Barney."

There was no urgent need to visit the house. What was to be found there had been found, or would be.

"Come on, Mullins," Bill Weigand said.

They went to dinner, first, and did not especially hurry over it. If occasion to hurry arose, which was not likely yet, they would be notified. They were not notified. They drove to the Elwell house. A uniformed policeman stood near the door and, as they approached, approached them—and then saw the badge Weigand held out to him and said, "Evening, sir."

"Visitors?" Weigand asked, and the patrolman shook his head.

"The man who works here came back," he said. "Little geezer named Higgins. Seems to be taking it hard."

Weigand rang and there was a pause—rather a long pause—and the door opened. Higgins was, as promised, a little geezer—a small man with not much gray hair, with sloping shoulders under a blue suit jacket, with a black string tie. His eyes were red.

" 'Iggins, sir," Delbert—the name no longer seemed so odd—Higgins said. "You've found out who killed him? Was it that Mr. Hunter?"

They didn't know yet, they said they didn't know yet.

"I should have been here," Delbert Higgins said, and his voice quavered. They were in the hallway by then, at the foot of stairs. "I'll never forgive myself, sir. Never as long as I live."

"Not your fault," Weigand said.

"It's easy to say that, sir," Higgins said. "All these years and when he needed me—" He shrugged sloping shoulders. "I'll carry it with me, sir," he said. "I suppose you want to go up there?"

They did.

"If you need me," Higgins said. "There's a bell to push. On the desk. He would ring and I'd—" He shook his head; said it just didn't seem possible, and his voice choked on the words.

They went up a flight and another flight, and into the large room with windows on the street, with a wide desk in front of the windows. A clock—a little silver clock—ticked on the desk. Not as sensitive as the clock in the song, obviously; not as suggestible. Why, Weigand wondered, had he thought of that word? He had, subconsciously, seen it at that instant—of course. On the back of a book. *Suggestibility in Children*. Elwell.

The room did not vary from the sketches of the room, from the photographs of the room. The desk—

with a blotter once pale green; not pale green now. A leather chair behind it and blood on the chair, too, as on the floor under it. Another leather chair at one end of the desk, and a typewriter (hooded) on a table against one wall, with a typist's chair in front of it. And a leather sofa and the door of the closet—

Weigand looked around the room, not touching anything. Sometimes, rooms seemed to speak, to remember. This room did not, so far as he could tell, have any comment to make—any comment not obvious. A man had been killed here; the blood told that. A man who worked at a desk, read books, wrote books.

Weigand tried the closet door. It was locked—a snap lock obviously. He had brought with him a chain of keys which had been among the personal effects of Professor Elwell, and selected one which looked appropriate and then the telephone rang. Mullins picked it up and said, "Mullins," and listened and said, "Hold it, I'll ask him."

"Picked up this guy Hunter," Mullins said. "Man who was here this afternoon? Want to know should they bring him here or—"

"Here," Weigand said.

"Bring him along," Mullins told the precinct.

The closet would wait. Weigand put the keys back in his pocket and looked for a button "on" the desk. It was set into the frame of the desk and he pushed it. After a little time they heard slow footsteps on the stairs; heard a knock at the door; opened the door to Delbert Higgins, who appeared to have been crying further, and to be a little breathless. Weigand waited, expectant. "You rang, sir?" Delbert Higgins said, satisfying expectation.

21

At a little after two he had admitted one Carl Hunter. At how much after two? Hunter was a frequent visitor. How frequent?

Perhaps five minutes after two, perhaps ten. Mr. Hunter came to see the professor a couple of times a week; usually, but not always, he came after dinner.

"He's what they call a graduate student, sir," Higgins said. "At least, that's what the professor told me. Working for his doctorate, the professor said. The professor was helping him, sir. People needed help, the professor would—" Higgins's voice broke; he dabbed his eyes. He said, "I'm sorry, sir. I'm not myself."

But probably, Bill Weigand thought, Higgins was himself, with a way of life suddenly cut off, no new way of life in sight. Bill said he understood. And Higgins himself had left—when?

About fifteen minutes after he had let Mr. Hunter in, and Hunter had climbed up toward the top-floor office. Higgins had heard the graduate student knock at the office door, had heard Professor Elwell say, "Come," and had gone down to his own quarters in the basement—"Although it really isn't that, sir. Very light and airy"—and changed his jacket and put on a topcoat and gone out through the service entrance in the rear and down two houses to a passageway to the street. And to a movie. And afterward—

"Never mind," Weigand said. "You locked the front door? The service door?"

"Certainly, sir."

"When Mr. Hunter went out—out the front door, presumably—it would have locked behind him? A snap lock, that is?"

"Oh yes, sir."

"You heard the professor ask Mr. Hunter to come in?"

"Oh yes, sir. 'Come,' the professor said. I heard that, sir."

"And nothing else?"

"Nothing—oh—no, *no* sir. You think I'd—"

"No," Weigand said. "Mr. Hunter's coming around, Higgins. With a man from the precinct. Let them in, will you?"

Higgins went. Bill Weigand took the keys out again, and again selected one appropriate and tried it in the closet door. The door opened. The closet was very shallow. Just depth enough to hold, on either side of the door, narrow filing cabinets, reaching to the ceiling. The rear wall of the closet was of wood. A closet hardly more than a niche in the wall, Weigand thought, as he closed the door and heard the tongue of the automatic lock snap into the slot of the striking plate. Of course, it would be in the exterior wall of the house. No depth possible unless it jutted into the house next door, which was unlikely. Odd that—

"Coming now," Mullins said, from the window and Weigand joined him there, and looked down at the top of a police car, at two men getting out of it. It was then, while they waited, that Weigand looked diagonally westward, and saw a slice of the Hudson in the moonlight.

And Carl Hunter, graduate student at Dyckman University, seeker after a doctorate in (it was to be assumed) psychology, came in and destroyed a small silver clock which had been, whatever he said, dutifully keeping time. . . .

"I could have sworn it was slow," Hunter said, in a puzzled voice. "Why else would I—" He stopped with that, and it was as if he had walked into a solid wall.

"When you were here this afternoon," Weigand said. "You saw the clock was slow then, Mr. Hunter? Was that the way it was?"

"That's it," Hunter said, relief in his tone. "Of course that's it. And the professor must have set—"

He stopped again.

"My God," he said. "We stand here and talk about—about a damn clock. And—*Jamey's dead. Killed.*"

"Right," Weigand said. "As I said, it must have happened soon after you left. When did you leave, Mr. Hunter?"

"I wasn't here more than half an hour," Hunter said. "So it must have been—oh, about a quarter of three."

"By the clock?"

"I don't think—no, I remember. By my watch. I looked at it and I had a—an appointment at three and I said, 'Thanks, sir,' and left. And he was all right, then. He was sitting right there"—Hunter pointed at the desk, and looked at it, and quickly looked away again—"and made a kind of salute, the way he did, and said, 'Don't keep her waiting, Carl' and—"

"Yes?" Bill Weigand said. "Her?"

"Just a girl I know," Hunter said.

"You met her—where was that?"

"At the Campus Book Store. Not that it's really on the campus. You see it's—"

"Never mind," Weigand said. "You met her—when, Mr. Hunter?"

"Well," Hunter said, and spoke slowly, "she was a little late, captain. It must have been—"

He did not, this time, hesitate to a stop. Sounds

stopped him—the sound of knocking stopped him, the snap of a lock.

A tall young woman—thin, almost gangling; a young woman with hair so blond as to be almost white—walked into the room and, seeing them, stopped—stopped with a kind of young awkwardness, as a child might stop who has chanced into a room forbidden children. Her face was thin; the blue eyes seemed too large for it. She put a thin hand up to her lips—to lips unexpectedly full, curved, bright.

But the reason Bill Weigand and Mullins stared at her was not related to her appearance. The reason was that the young woman had walked out of the closet.

2

Bill Weigand looked from the young woman to Sergeant Aloysius Mullins, and looked by instinct and with sympathy. Events were baffling enough to Weigand; what, he thought, must they be to Mullins? A look told him.

It was not so much surprise that flooded over Sergeant Mullins's large, always somewhat reddened, face. Surprise was there, of course—surprise, disbelief, even consternation. But under those things, the basis of those things, was a great indignation, a great anger. This, Mullins's face said, was beyond acceptance. This went too far—this went a helluva lot too far. This—

"All right, sergeant," Bill Weigand said, gently, and turned back to the girl, who was looking from one to the other of them, eyes very round—very startled. But when she spoke, it was to Carl Hunter. Her voice was unexpectedly low, vibrant.

"Carl," she said. "Carl—what is it? What's happened?"

"Screwy," Sergeant Mullins said, in a faraway voice. "That's what it is—screwy."

But it was clear that he spoke only to himself, a man withdrawn from that which could not be tolerated.

"Where's Uncle Jamey?" the girl said.

"Faith—" Carl Hunter said but, instead of going on, looked at Weigand, left it to him.

"I'm sorry," Weigand said. "Professor Elwell is dead. He was—shot." He looked at the desk and the girl looked and then raised both hands to her thin face and covered her face, and the tips of her slim fingers rubbed against her forehead, as if to lessen sudden pain. They waited. After a few seconds the tall girl lowered her hands. Her eyes seemed more than ever too large for her thin, now very pale, face.

"Your uncle?" Bill Weigand said.

For an instant she looked at him as if she had not heard him, almost as if she did not see him. But then she shook her head.

"Not really," she said. "I called him that. Always. Since I was a little girl. Killed? Just—sitting there and somebody shot him?"

Some things must be repeated before they become real.

"Yes," Bill Weigand said.

"I'm Faith Oldham," the girl said. "We live downstairs."

"Down—" Bill began, and did not finish. Instead he went past the girl to the closet. She had left the door partly open and he opened it more widely. Of course— it should all along have been obvious. Not a closet, really—not primarily a closet. A passage into the house next door. What he had taken to be the back wall of the closet was a door. Yes—a sliding door,

27

open now. He went through into the house next door, into a room which, in size and shape, was a twin of the professor's office. But not in furnishing—this other room was carpeted, as the office was not; here heavy curtains were drawn across the windows. There was faint illumination in the room from a ceiling light. Weigand went back into the room Elwell had died in.

"Downstairs in the other house?" Bill said to the girl, who looked at him as if the question surprised her but then said, "Yes. Of course. My mother and I—"

It was not, once explained, in any special way remarkable. Jameson Elwell had owned two houses, side by side, shoulder to shoulder and wall to wall. He occupied all of one and the top floor of the other, and had had a passage opened through and used the double thickness of the two house walls as storage space. And the curtained room?

"He called it the laboratory," Carl Hunter said. "Carried on—experiments. Psychological experiments. Psychological—enquiries."

"I see," Bill said, but was not sure he did see. "With animals?"

"Animals?" Hunter repeated. The girl merely stood and looked at Hunter. "Oh—you're thinking of Pavlov? Thorndike? No. That is, not here. That's done at the university. We've got a project now with cats that may—" He stopped and shook his head impatiently. "Which is neither here nor there," he said. "This—I suppose the word 'laboratory' gives the wrong impression to a layman. A room to talk to people in. A—quiet room." He looked at Weigand sharply. "Nothing mysterious," he said. "And certainly nothing to do with what's happened."

The uneasiness, the uncertainty, had gone from Carl Hunter's manner. He seemed now quite sure of himself. Too sure, at least of the point he made. There was no telling, yet, what it had to do or did not have to do with what had happened.

For one thing, it was evident that Higgins's locking of the service door, the automatic locking of the front door when Hunter went out of it—if he had, whenever he had—proved nothing one way or the other. Clearly, anyone—including a murderer—might get from one house to the other through the "laboratory." As Faith Oldham just had.

"Miss Oldham," Weigand said. "It is *Miss* Oldham?"

She looked at him, now, but as if she had returned from a long journey.

"Oh," she said. "Yes. Miss."

"Did Professor Elwell expect you this evening?"

"Expect—oh. There wasn't anything definite. When—when I want to see him I come through the other room and knock and if he's not busy—" She put her fingers to her curved, full lips. "That's the way it—used to be," she said, the low voice muffled.

"You come—?" Bill said, and his voice was almost as low as the girl's.

"When—when I want to ask him something," she said. "When I'm worried. He's like—he was like—I don't know. He knew so much. Was so—kind."

A childlike quality persisted. Then, abruptly, it vanished.

"Who killed him?" she said, and her tone demanded. "Why would anybody kill him?"

"I don't know," Weigand said. "It only happened a

29

few hours ago. Apparently, just after Mr. Hunter left him. Did he say anything about expecting someone, Mr. Hunter? Another student, perhaps?"

"Don't you think I'd have told you if he had?" Hunter said. "No."

"And you," Weigand said. "You came to ask him something too, Mr. Hunter?"

"No," Hunter said. "The other way around. This project—no use going into that. He was supervising it, of course. A lot of us are doing the spade work. I brought him some tabulations to check over. One of us—usually I was the one—brought him data two or three times a week."

"Look," Mullins said, "what did you say this project was about? Did you say cats, mister?"

Bill did not quite smile. It was so evident that Mullins hoped, hoped anxiously, that the project was not about cats. But Hunter and the girl merely looked, a little blankly, at the large sergeant.

"Why?" Hunter said. "Yes. It's about cats. Their varying reactions to stimuli under—" He snapped his fingers. "Don't start me on that," he said. "Why?"

"Cats," Mullins repeated. He spoke as a man whose worst fears have been confimed. Men broke clocks, young women came out of closets and now—cats. Omens.

"Another screwy one," Sergeant Mullins said, as much to himself as to Captain William Weigand.

"They're not in it," Weigand said, gently.

"They will be," Mullins told him. Mullins spoke from an abyss.

Hunter and Faith Oldham looked from one policeman to the other.

"This girl you were going to meet at the bookshop," Weigand said to Hunter. "You said she was late?"

"Carl," the girl said. "I—I told you. I couldn't—"

"Never mind," Hunter said, and smiled at the tall girl and there was, Bill thought, warmth and reassurance in his smile and—and more? There was no use guessing.

"How late were you, Miss Oldham?" Bill asked her.

"About twenty minutes," she said. "It was supposed to be three o'clock and—*Carl. Does it matter?*"

"Jamey was killed a little after three, they say," Carl Hunter told her. "If we'd been together at the bookshop—" He shrugged.

The tall girl turned on Weigand. Her face was not pale now. Her face was flushed. She was quite a different person now from the tall, uneasy girl who had walked into the room and stopped, abashed.

"You're not crazy enough to think Carl—Carl knows anything about this," she said. "Nobody could be that—"

"Wait," Bill said. "Mr. Hunter's ahead of us. He was here this afternoon. Of course we have to find out what we can about when he left. And—"

She did not wait.

"What you're saying," she said, "is that he needs an alibi. Isn't that what you're saying?"

Her tone accused.

"I—" Weigand began, but was interrupted. Sergeant Mullins had returned.

"Lady," Sergeant Mullins said, and spoke to a child. "A good alibi never hurt anybody. Whether he needs it or don't need it."

"For the record," Hunter said, "I didn't kill Professor Jameson Elwell."

"Right," Bill said. "Now—about this laboratory. Let's have a look at it."

He led them into it, pausing long enough to confirm the obvious—that the door into the office, from the "closet" which was only incidentally a closet, could be locked against entrance from the office, but not against entrance to the office. Which seemed at first a little odd, but did not a moment later. To get into the "laboratory" from the other house one needed a key. Weigand opened that door, looked at the top of a flight of stairs and closed the door again.

"You have a key, of course," he told Faith Oldham. "Anybody else you know of? Your mother?"

"No," she said. "I don't know about anybody else. Uncle Jamey gave me a key so I could—if I needed to talk to him I mean—come this way instead of going outside and up through the other house and—" She stopped. "I don't know about any other keys," she said.

"The door downstairs," Bill said. "The front door. Of this house. It's kept locked, of course?"

"Yes," she said. "I don't—oh, you mean somebody could have got in through our house? I don't mean ours, really—it was his house. Mother and I just—rent the lower floors. That's what you mean?"

"Yes," Bill said. "If somebody had a key to the front door, another key to this door"—he pointed—"he could come up without you or your mother seeing him? Or—hearing him?"

How, she wanted to know, could she answer that? It depended on where they were in the house. On whether they were in the house at all. This afternoon, for example—this afternoon she had left the house at about three to meet Hunter at the bookshop. Her mother had been there at the time, but had been dressed to go out, ready to go out. When she had actually gone only she could tell them. "But she's not home now," Faith Oldham said. "This is her bridge night."

"Servants?"

She smiled at that, smiled faintly. "Not for a long time," Faith Oldham said. "Not for years and years. You see, daddy—" She stopped. She shook her head, as if at herself. "Look," she said. "I told you we rented our part of the house. We—well, we don't. Uncle Jamey just lets—just let—us live there. Because he and daddy—Anyway, that's the way it is. And—that's the way he—was."

It had taken effort, Bill Weigand thought. It had taken honesty.

"After you two met," he said. "At the bookshop. At around twenty minutes after three—" He waited a moment. Hunter nodded his head and the nod said, All right so far.

He had moved a little closer to the girl.

"What did you do the rest of the afternoon?"

"I don't see—" Hunter said and looked with raised eyebrows at Bill Weigand, who did not precisely see either, except that one does not press always at a single spot. "Went to a lecture—lecture on contemporary drama—at the Hartley Theater. That's part of the university, you know." He seemed to doubt Weigand did. "Right," Bill said.

"Lasted an hour and a half," Carl Hunter said. "Or

thereabouts. Beginning at four. Then—well, we walked around for a while and talked for a while, and went to a place and had a drink and then—well, then, Faith had to go home. And I went back to watch the cats."

He looked at Mullins when he said that. Mullins did not look at him.

Faith Oldham had come home; she had "helped" with the dinner. Her mother had been home then. At about eight her mother had gone toward bridge. Faith had washed up, and read a while and then—

"There was something I wanted to ask Uncle Jamey," she said and then covered her face again and her thin shoulders began to shake. And Carl Hunter went to her and put an arm around her shoulders, and held her.

"Listen," he said, "that's all we know."

"Right," Bill said, not knowing whether it was right or not, but only that there are times to press and times to give. "If anything else comes up—"

Which let them go. They went, together, toward the door. "By the way," Bill said, as they neared it, "I think I'd better take the key, Miss Oldham. You won't have any more use for it. And we like—"

She brought the key back to him. She did not say anything.

"So?" Hunter said.

"Good night," Bill said. "We'll know where to find you, if we need to."

As, he thought, when the door closed behind them—the girl was almost as tall as Hunter—they probably would.

"Why laboratory?" Mullins said, as they looked around the room. "No test tubes." He looked up at the ceiling. "Now that's something," he said. "Acoustic ceiling. And the curtains and carpet and all."

Bill nodded. A room built for silence, for concentration. And, certainly, with no test tubes. A laboratory of the mind, if one at all.

A desk, not as large as the one in the office. A leather couch with a table beside it and, on the table, a tape recorder. A chair beside the couch. Across the room, a table phonograph. At the end of the room most distant from the windows, two doors. Bill indicated them with his head and Mullins opened one, which led to a bathroom. He opened the other, which opened on a corridor. Mullins went down the corridor and, almost at once, returned.

"One other room," he said. "Just used it as a storeroom, from the looks of things. Loot, this is a screwy one."

"That record's stuck, sergeant," Bill said, and grinned at Mullins who said, "Maybe. But all the same—"

"Speaking of records," Bill said, "we'll want to take that along." He indicated the recorder.

"Sure," Mullins said. "We run the tape and somebody says, 'My name is Joseph Q. Zilch. I am now gonna kill you, professor, on account of' and then, pretty soon, *bang!* And we go out and arrest Zilch and he says, 'You got me, pals.' Only, do we ever get nice simple ones, Loot?"

"No," Bill said. "Does anybody?"

He was abstracted. He looked around the room again. He had, he thought, seldom seen two less communicative rooms than the office and the laboratory of the late Professor Elwell. He went over and looked at the record player and found a record on it.

Mullins stood and watched him. Bill set the turntable revolving and the stylus arm rose obediently, hesitated, settled.

"Please listen carefully to what I say," a man's voice said. The voice was low, the words spoken slowly; the voice soothed. There was a momentary pause. "That's right," the voice said. "That is precisely right. Now this is what I would like you to do. This is what I would like you to do. Stand easily—that is right. Relax. That is right. Close your eyes, now. Close your eyes. Close your eyes."

The voice was infinitely soothing. There was soft assurance in the low male voice.

"Now," the voice said, "you will begin to feel yourself falling slowly forward—forward—you are falling slowly forward—forward—forward. You are beginning to lose your balance—something is pulling you slowly—slowly—slowly—forward. You are falling slowly forward. But do not try to resist—you cannot resist—you are falling forward—forward—there is nothing to be afraid of—I will catch you—you are falling forward, slowly forward—an irresistible force is slowly pulling you forward—you cannot help yourself but I will not let you fall—I will catch you—forward—forward you are falling slowly—falling—falling—"

It was soothing, relaxing. It was as, when one has taken a sleeping pill, gradually, tenderly, sleep creeps—creeps—

"The hell with this," Bill Weigand thought, with something like anger, and opened his eyes—and was startled because he could not remember having closed his eyes.

"Forward," the soft voice said. "Forward. You are falling slowly forward—you cannot—"

36

The hell I can't, Bill Weigand thought, now with clear anger. And looked at Sergeant Mullins.

Sergeant Mullins, eyes closed as directed, heels together, arms hanging loosely, was standing in the middle of the room. And Sergeant Mullins was swaying slowly, contentedly, forward and back, forward and back; nodding like the mast of a sailboat in a gently rolling sea.

It was ludicrous. It was also, in some odd fashion, disturbing, even alarming.

Weigand lifted the player arm and the voice stopped. Mullins stopped swaying. He did not, however, open his eyes.

"Mullins!" Bill Weigand said, sharply.

Mullins opened his eyes.

"What kind of record is that?" Mullins said. "Damnedest thing I ever heard."

"Yes," Bill said. "It is an odd sort of record."

"All this stuff about falling," Mullins said. "Who's going to pay any attention to that? If this professor thought anybody was going to think he was falling forward, forward, forward like it said, then the professor was nuts."

Bill Weigand looked at Sergeant Mullins for a moment with speculation. Then he said, "Right, sergeant. Very silly business," and took the record off the player and examined it. It had no title. It was scored only on one side. He would, Bill decided, have to take advice about the record on Professor Elwell's turntable.

It was, among other things, interesting that Sergeant Mullins apparently had no realization whatever that he had obeyed the reiterated injunction and stood swaying gently, but always, it appeared, with the assurance

37

that he would be caught, in the middle of a room built for silence.

It was unfortunate that Professor Jameson Elwell was dead, and so could not tell them what it was all about. He would have to ask somebody else. That, perhaps, was the next step.

Technicians worked in Professor Elwell's laboratory, collected its dust and its fingerprints, took its picture and measured its walls. Mullins and precinct men and a detective assigned to the district attorney's Homicide Bureau, listened to the tape from the recorder—listened to it from end to end, and heard only the faint scratching of a blank tape. (Not, then, a nice simple one, as Mullins had supposed it would not be.)

Then Mullins, with precinct aid, began the long, necessary chore of checking back on those they already knew about—on Mrs. Oldham and daughter, Faith; on Carl Hunter, graduate student obscurely concerned with cats; on such others as might appear. One of the others—Foster Elwell, brother of deceased—ought soon to appear, unless he was walking in from Westport. He would be asked to await the return of Captain Weigand.

Bill Weigand, meanwhile, had driven twenty blocks to the north, and found Dr. Eugene Wahmsley, dean of faculty, Dyckman University, waiting for him in the Men's Faculty Club, as promised on the telephone. Dr. Wahmsley was a tanned man in his fifties, who looked as if he might play a good deal of golf. He got up from a deep leather chair and shook hands and said it was a shocking thing about poor Jamey and added that his loss would be felt.

"A great man in his field," Dr. Wahmsley said, and

although what he said was obvious he said it as if he meant it. He motioned Weigand to a chair, sat again in his own. A silver coffee pot stood on a table by his chair, beside an empty coffee cup and a half-empty pony glass of brandy. Dr. Wahmsley lifted the coffee pot and shook it and then shook his head, and then gestured. A man in a waiter's jacket appeared. Dr. Wahmsley looked at the coffee pot with reproach.

"More coffee," he said. "And a Courvoisier for my guest."

"I—" Bill said.

"And tell them to make sure it's fresh coffee," Dr. Wahmsley said, with some sternness. "Yes, captain?"

"Nothing," Bill said. Coffee and brandy seemed, on second thought, an excellent idea.

"You want to know about Jamey," Wahmsley told him. "I gather it wasn't some ordinary thing? Interrupted robbery, some young hood—that sort of thing?"

"It doesn't seem so," Bill told him, and told him what he needed to know—which was about as much as Bill knew himself—about the manner of Jameson Elwell's death. Wahmsley said that it was hard to believe. Bill told him that murder always was.

"A bit of psychologist yourself, I gather," Wahmsley said, and thanked the waiter for more coffee and watched it poured. "I said Jamey was a great man in his field," Wahmsley said then. "What one always says, of course. About him, it happens to be true. You know anything about his work?"

"No," Bill said. "Oh, that he was professor of psychology, that he was supervising some sort of an experiment which involved cats—that he had a room in his house—the house next door, actually, but I gather he owned it—that he called a laboratory. In brief—nothing of importance about his work." He sipped. "Or at the moment," he added, "about any part of him."

"Animal intelligence," Wahmsley said. "That explains the cats. We feel here that he carried on—a long distance on—from where Thorndike and the rest left off." He looked at Weigand with sudden doubt. "Edward Lee Thorndike?" he said.

"I've heard of Thorndike," Bill said, with no special inflection. "I went to Columbia for a time."

"Good school," Wahmsley said. "Very good school. Well—that explains the cats. Also, a number of dogs and even more rats and quite a few monkeys."

He poured himself more coffee.

"A great researcher in his field," Wahmsley said, and seemed to speak to the silver coffee pot, and spoke slowly. "A great teacher. And—more than that." He looked at Weigand now. "A very special sort of man," he said. "Aside from all that. It is—to be honest, captain, it seems flatly impossible that anybody would kill a man like Elwell. Anybody in his right mind. Or what passes for rightness of mind nowadays."

"Nevertheless," Bill Weigand said. "But go on, doctor. A special sort of man?"

Dr. Wahmsley regarded the silver coffee pot for some seconds.

"In understanding," he said, finally, and spoke with deliberation, as if seeking words. "In a sense, of course, trying to understand the way the mind works was his trade. I don't mean only that. More than anyone else I've ever known he went beyond the mere technics of understanding. It was as if he—" Dr.

Wahmsley shared his hesitancy with the silver coffee pot "—went into the minds of others, shared what was in other minds. With the utmost sympathy, the most complete—generosity. Perhaps that is the word I want. Generosity. Not only in the obvious sense."

He shook his head at the silver coffee pot and seemed, Bill thought, to shake it in reproof as if the coffee pot had failed him. Then he said that it was difficult to put into words precisely what he meant. He added that words were elusive things and asked if Captain Weigand had not found it so.

"Yes," Bill said. "They turn up meaning more, or less, than we intend. But—an unusually generous man."

"And—understanding," Wahmsley said. "Sympathetic. Use all the usual words. Barnacled with associations, worn smooth with usage. There—you see what we come to? Roughened by accretions, at the same time, worn smooth."

He was, Bill thought, again in conversation with the coffee pot.

"In the most simple word," he said, to the pot. "A good man. Which means much less than it should. But—not the kind of man who is killed by another man or a woman. I would have sworn that. I have always felt that getting oneself murdered must result from a flaw somewhere—a flaw in character. Almost as much as murdering."

He looked at the coffee pot again. He told the silver pot that he talked like a professor. He told Bill Weigand that he was sorry to be wasting so much of his time. He told Bill that Bill wanted facts and—

Professor Elwell had been on the Dyckman faculty for something like forty years, starting as an instructor while still working for his master's, his doctorate. He had gone up the slow, but reasonably sure, steps—assistant professor, associate, full professor, head of department. (The last step, of course, by no means inevitable.) He would have reached the retirement age in a few months. "Technically," Dr. Wahmsley pointed out. "No real difference, if he chose not to have any. Oh—no further administrative duties, of course. But everything else much as before."

"I take it," Bill said, "that he had money of his own. Beyond his salary."

"My God yes," Wahmsley said, in honest astonishment. "You pointed out yourself he owned two houses. He was a college professor, man."

"About his generosity," Bill said. "You said 'not only in the obvious sense.' I suppose you meant not only with money? But—included that."

"Well," Wahmsley said, "we've a term around here—So-and-so's probably on an 'Elwell scholarship.' We had to guess, for the most part. Jamey wouldn't mention anything like that, and most of the kids were—well, I suppose, asked not to. But—likely kids who came along without money and looked like having to drop out rather often discovered they didn't need to. Because of Jamey."

He was asked if he wanted to name names. He said he didn't, at least unless the captain could assure him that names would help. He said, also, that most names he might give would be guessed at.

"A man named Hunter?" Bill asked him. "A girl named Faith Oldham?"

"Hunter?" Wahmsley repeated. "We have fifteen thousand students here—in the college, in the schools, in the whole setup. I'd guess a hundred Hunters, wouldn't you? As for the Oldham child. That's quite a different matter. She's Frank Oldham's daughter." He seemed to feel that he had said all that needed saying. Bill lifted his shoulders.

"Sic transit," Wahmsley said. "A philosopher of some note, we felt. A pride of Dyckman. And, a great friend of Jamey's. His closest, oldest, I imagine. A man of great wisdom, Frank was. But—improvident as they come. So when he died ten years ago or so—and left a widow and a young daughter—and nothing else to speak of—" He ended with a gesture.

Bill Weigand said he saw.

"In Elwell's—what he seems to have called his laboratory," Bill said. "We came across a rather odd phonograph record. I don't know whether you can help on—"

" 'Forward'?" Wahmsley said. " 'You are falling slowly forward' and the rest of it?"

"Right."

"Just a sway test record," Wahmsley said, as if so much (at least) should have been obvious. "Gauges susceptibility to hypnosis. Or's supposed to. Not my field."

"Elwell's?"

"Oh," Wahmsley said. "Very much his field. Very much indeed. A field of increasing importance, you know. Now that the medical profession isn't so afraid of it. Jamey's last publication made quite a stir, I understand. Boys over at the press are a bit green about it."

To that Bill Weigand could only shake a bewildered head.

"Dyckman University Press," Wahmsley said, spelling it out. "Jealousy, green with. Jamey gave it to a trade publisher, to get wider circulation. Some of the public's still a bit stuffy about the whole subject, you know. Or, say uninformed."

"Doctor," Bill Weigand said. "Do you happen to know who published this last book of Professor Elwell's?"

He waited the answer with somewhat bated mind. It happened that Dr. Wahmsley did know.

Bill Weigand was not really much surprised. Mullins had a good policeman's feel for the shape of things, including those to come.

3

It had been what Pamela North sometimes thinks of as a "why-not?" evening, which she regards as often the best kind of evening. It had begun, as such evenings frequently do, with cocktails. That idea had been Dorian Weigand's, who reported, on the telephone to Pam, that she felt like seeing people, and that Bill, the evening before had asked her whatever had become of the Norths.

"In ten days?" Pam said to that. "Not that it wasn't a very nice thing for him to say. Why not here, though?"

Which was the first of the "why-nots?" and an impermanent one since, as Dorian pointed out, it was her idea. And it would be good for Bill, who had had precisely the sort of day he found most arduous—a day hanging about General Sessions, waiting to be called as a witness. The Norths would cheer him.

"You'd think," Pam said, when later she learned that Bill would not be present to be cheered, "you'd

45

think Inspector O'Malley knew we were coming."

The idea was, admittedly, a bit slippery. Dorian and Jerry looked at each other. Jerry North shrugged, elaborately. "You make me tired," Pam said. "Both of you. You know how O'Malley feels about us, although I can't think why, because mostly we help. So, if he knew we were coming, it would be just like him to do a thing like this."

"Listen," Jerry North said, and ran his fingers through his hair. "Listen, Pam. You mean, I mean you don't mean, that the inspector arranged to have somebody murdered so that Bill would have to work and couldn't come home for cocktails because we were going to be here?"

"You certainly make things sound complicated," Pam told him, with wide-eyed innocence.

It was around six, then. It was around seven-thirty when Pam said, "Why not come out to dinner with us? Since Bill isn't here, and we have to because Martha likes Wednesday better than Thursday." Dorian and Jerry waited. "To be off on," Pam said.

It was a little before nine when they finished dinner. "As long as we're up and about," Jerry said, "why not go look at that movie at the Art? The actress with the—"

"I know," Pam said. "The one with both of them rather—extravagantly. 'The,' indeed."

Jerry said that his interest, actually, lay elsewhere and realized, from the pleased expression on the faces of both Pam and Dorian, that he had not greatly improved matters. He said, "Anyway—" which was as useful a remark as he could think of, and they went to the movie. From it, they walked, cross town, to the apartment house in which the Weigands lived.

"Why not," Dorian said, "come up for a nightcap? Maybe Bill's home by now."

They went up for a nightcap. It was a "why-not?" evening.

The telephone was ringing in the apartment—which has a view of more than a slice of the East River; for several reasons, all quite legal, the Weigands do not live on a policeman's salary—when Dorian opened the door. She was across the room to it, moving as if en route from base-line to net position. She said into it, "Darling!" and then, "At a movie, with the Norths; don't sound like a cop, darling" and then, "Yes, they did as it happens." And then listened.

"I'm sure they will," Dorian said, and turned toward Pam and Jerry and twisted the receiver away from her lips, "Won't you?" she said.

"Of course," Pam North said, with no hesitation. "We'd love to."

"I'm not so—" Dorian said, and then, into the telephone now, "Yes, Bill?" and again listened. She said, "All right. Ten minutes," and put the receiver back.

"So nice he wants us to—" Pam began and stopped, seeing Dorian's face.

"Of course he does," Dorian said. "Only—well, this time there's something more to it. It seems the man who was killed was somebody you publish, Jerry. A Professor Elwell, and—"

"No!" Pam said. *"Not Jamey!"*

But there was no use saying it was not Jamey, no use saying it couldn't be, that it didn't make sense, as Pam did to Bill, when he arrived as promised. It could be because it was; making sense out of it was, Bill Weigand hoped, where the Norths might help.

"Sometimes," Pam said, a little later, "it seems as if there's no future in being a North author. There was that dinosaur man and—"

They knew. Several authors published by North Books, Inc., have led troubled lives, abruptly terminated. A poet once, and a novelist, and of course the dinosaur man. Pam has moments, but they pass quickly, of thinking that it might have been better if they had not found their first body in a bathtub or, having found it, left it unmentioned.

It was not, Jerry told Bill, on being asked, odd that North Books, instead of a publisher of scientific works, should have brought out Elwell's *Hypnotism in the Modern World*. For one thing, the book had been written for the lay reader. For another, Jerry, hearing about the book through a friend of his at Dyckman— "a scout, if you must know"—had gone after it.

"Why?" Bill asked.

"Because," Jerry told him, "we like to sell books."

Bill waited that one out.

"In the last year or so," Jerry said, "there's been— well, a resurgence of interest in hypnotism. And, in the acceptance of hypnotism. It's been a long time coming, especially in the United States."*

"Because, Jamey always said, of vaudeville," Pam said. "The mumbo jumbo. And doctors, even the ones who knew about it, didn't use it much—or maybe admit using it—because people think of men in capes and glittering eyes." She paused. "And stiff people

---

* "Organized medicine in the United States has taken more than a century to accept the use of hypnosis. At last, the American Medical Association has reported (in its September 1958 Journal) that hypnosis 'has a recognized place' in the medical armory, including surgery."—*Harper's* Magazine, November, 1958.

between chairs," she added. "Jamey says—" She stopped, abruptly. "Jerry!" she said. "He was—such a *lamb*. How anybody—"

"I know," Jerry said, and then, to Bill, "That's about it. Recently, because of the work of men like Elwell and a lot of others—the notion that there's some kind of black magic about it, or that it isn't true at all, has begun to break down. With medical men, where it's important. With laymen. It took a long time to make most people accept that the earth isn't flat."

Bill said that Jerry seemed, more or less overnight so far as he could see, to have become unexpectedly familiar with hypnosis. Jerry grinned at that, said he was a quick study, that he read the books he published.

"Also," he said, "Jamey had a way of—of making things exciting." He paused, spoke more slowly. "He was quite a guy, Bill," Jerry said. "I feel pretty much the same way Pam does."

They had known Jameson Elwell only for three or four months, but had, increasingly, seen more of him than the author-publisher relationship fully explained. That sometimes happened. Sometimes it was all business, now and then even rather scratchy business. ("These damn subsidiaries," Jerry said, somewhat obscurely, and in passing.) Sometimes, an author was as good as his book, or even, on occasion, better. "We hit it off," Jerry said. "He and I first and then Pam heard about the cats. At first, at lunch, very casually. She had been—"

"I got to talking about Martini," Pam said. "And poor Sherry. And poor Gin. And any son—" She looked at Jerry, who had said nothing. "All right," she said, "any *man* who doesn't cover an abandoned well.

And then about cats in general." She paused, considered. "I do," she said, "talk a good deal about cats, I guess. And Jamey told us about—"

He had told them about the cats into whose elusive, surprising minds he and several others were peering at Dyckman University. He had taken Pam to see the cats—

"Doing all sorts of things," Pam said. "In and out of boxes and stepping on things to make things happen and—"

She had been worried, at first, having come to like Jameson Elwell and being afraid that, if he was doing the wrong things to cats, she wouldn't any more. But the cats had all seemed very happy, to be enjoying themselves. "Cats *like* to do things," Pam said. "Especially when they're young."

She stopped and said again that she did talk a good deal about cats. "Actually," she said, "Jamey used dogs, too, and monkeys. And elephants at one time, I think. But, elephants do take up space, of course."

This was commemorated by a moment of silence.

"I doubt," Jerry said, "if elephants come into it, particularly. I don't know what we can tell you, Bill. The book's going well. We've been to his house—a couple of times for dinner. He showed us his laboratory—he did some hypnosis experiments there—started that when Dyckman was still leery enough to prefer to have them done off campus. It's changed its mind now. You found the laboratory room?"

Bill had. He told them about the record.

"A quick way," Jerry said, "to find out whether a person can be hypnotized—will go into somnambulistic trance. Only about one in five will, according to

Elwell. Listening to the record, good subjects will begin to sway back and forth and—" He stopped, on looking at Bill Weigand's face. "Don't," Jerry said, "tell me *you* swayed, Bill. Nothing against it—apparently the more intelligent, the more sensitive, a person is the better chance—"

"Thanks," Bill said. "But, no." He hesitated a moment. "I haven't told him," Bill said. "And don't you. But—Mullins swayed just fine. And—didn't know he was doing it."

He looked enquiringly at Jerry, who said he wasn't the authority, just a man who had published an authority. But it seemed probable. At least, people in hypnosis didn't remember, when they came out of it, were brought out of it, that they had been in. Or, needn't, unless the operator wanted them to. Jerry said that there were wrinkles within wrinkles, and that he would send Bill a copy of Elwell's book.

"Long book?" Bill asked, with evident doubt. "All right—no need to look like a Cheshire cat."

Jerry, still looking rather like one (except that he did not leave his grin hanging in mid-air), said that Professor Elwell's book was, perhaps, rather long. "People seem to like long books nowadays," Jerry said. "Apparently long books give them a sense of—" He paused. "Completion, maybe."

"Accomplishment," Pam said. "They get through and say, 'My. Look what I did.' Particularly novels, of course. The kinds with heroines."

"Carl Hunter?" Bill said, bringing them back. The Norths looked at him, at each other; they shook heads.

"Should we?" Pam asked.

"A graduate student," Bill said. "Working with Elwell on the animal psychology experiments." They shook their heads again.

"He was there this afternoon," Bill told them. "Left before the professor was killed. He says."

They waited.

"I have no idea," Bill said. "It's obviously possible. You remember a little silver clock the professor had on the desk in his office?"

"You do jump around," Pam said. "Clock? Don't tell me it stopped when the—when Jamey died?"

"Not then," Bill said, and told them when, and how, the clock too had died.

"What a funny thing for somebody to do," Pam said. "Because the clock—was slow? But, you say it wasn't. Was Mullins there? Say it was screwy?"

"Yes," Bill said. "He did use the expression—later and in general terms. He was a little puzzled that you two weren't—that is."

"I know," Pam said. "Poor Mullins. His worst hopes. A clock phobia? I mean—some people go in for clocks, which is supposed to mean something. Do some people go—out for clocks?" She looked at her husband. "Jerry's thinking," she said.

The three of them—Dorian quiet, live-eyed, curled in a chair—looked at Gerald North expectantly.

"In hypnotism," he said, "there's a—wrinkle. Seems that, during a trance, the operator can tell the subject that, after he comes out of it—at a certain time afterward—he will do a certain thing. Won't be able to help doing it. Have an irresistible impulse. Usually, of course, to do something that doesn't make any sense. Afterward, they usually rationalize. Make up reasons for doing the nonsensical thing." He paused. "I wish you'd read the book yourself," he said to Bill. "If you think hypnotism has anything to do with—with Jamey's death."

"I doubt if it—" Bill began.

"It seems," Dorian said, "like a devious way to get a clock broken. If you mean that this Mr. Hunter was acting under posthypnotic suggestion."

Now they looked at Dorian.

"Oh," she said, "I read. That's what you were thinking about, wasn't it, Jerry?"

It seemed possible, Jerry said. If Elwell was right, and he had no doubt that Elwell had been right. "To be honest," Jerry said, "I had a couple of other experts check the book. In some aspects, they said, very original. In all aspects, very sound. Where was I?"

"Possible," Pam said. "About the clock."

Oh—that Hunter, hypnotized, had been told that, at a certain time—or perhaps when he was next in the office—he would take the clock off the desk and throw it into the fireplace. Assuming, of course, that he had been a subject of Elwell's hypnotic experiments. Assuming that Elwell didn't mind having the clock broken.

"Why?" Dorian said. "Why would the professor arrange something that would end in—breaking something? It seems—wanton."

They all, again, regarded Jerry North, who said, "Listen. All I know is what I've read in Jamey's book. Of course—"

They waited.

As he understood it, Jerry said, there was considerable scientific uncertainty as to just how far a person could be persuaded to go under hypnosis. At one time, it was generally—almost universally—believed that a subject could not be swayed to do anything which he would, awake, consider wrong. But experimenters were no longer so sure of that; certainly were not sure within a certain zone.

It was conceivable—always assuming that Hunter had been a subject of experimentation ("Which would have to have been with his full consent; they're still pretty sure of that.")—it was conceivable that Professor Elwell had been exploring that particular zone. The average normal person does not, wantonly as Dorian had said, destroy the property of others, especially property of any value. As presumably the clock had been?

"I'd think so," Bill told him.

Then, Elwell might have given Hunter the posthypnotic suggestion—instruction—that he destroy the clock, to see how far Hunter could be got to go.

"We could ask Hunter himself," Bill said. "Or—would he know?"

That was difficult to answer; for that answer they needed somebody who really knew something about the subject. If Carl Hunter had been an active participant, rather than merely a passive subject, in the experiments—if he was himself something of an expert—he might recognize his destruction of the clock as a result of posthypnotic suggestion. He might recognize that, and still rationalize by contending that the clock was worthless, running slow. Or, it might be that the suggestion had included the explanation—that Elwell had himself, during Hunter's hypnosis, offered the worthlessness of the clock as a means of breaking down, in advance, Hunter's block against vandalism.

"Phew," Jerry North said, and went to the sideboard and mixed himself a moderate drink.

"We'll ask, probably," Bill said. "After I read this damned book. At Elwell's—did you meet a tall, pale girl, a girl with very large blue eyes, named Faith? Faith Oldham?"

"The poor child," Pam said. "Yes."

"Poor?"

"Who," Pam said, "wants to be named Faith? It was revenge, really. Her mother's named Hope, you know. Got her own back. She's very nice, though—Faith, I mean. Not bitter or anything that I could see. Jamey was very fond of her. Treated her—well, as if she were his own daughter. Don't tell me she—"

Bill was not, he pointed out, telling her anything. Faith Oldham could have got to Elwell's office without going through the—call it the main house. So, conceivably, given a key, could almost anyone else. Faith and Carl Hunter were, at the least, good friends.

"She felt toward Jamey," Pam said, "as if he were her father. I'm sure—" She stopped, considered. "No," she said. "I'm *really* sure." She looked at Jerry. "And," she said, "we'll have no loose talk of intuition, of either sex."

"As a matter of fact," Jerry said, "I feel the way Pam does. Without, of course, being able to prove it. You know about his own daughter—Elizabeth, her name was? She was killed in a car accident before we met Elwell. And—"

"Yes," Bill said. "We know about her. You mean that, after that, Elwell in a sense adopted Faith Oldham? Emotionally, I mean?"

They didn't know. It seemed possible.

The telephone rang. "Oh dear," Dorian said, and went across the room to answer it. She said, "All right, sergeant," and beckoned with the handpiece.

"Only," Dorian told her husband, as he took the telephone from her, "remember that even detectives have to sleep sometime."

He nodded. He said, "Yes, sergeant?" and then, for some time without saying anything further, listened.

"Right," he said, finally. "The morning will do. Tell him, around nine-thirty. And I'll meet him at the club. Have somebody check out the accident Elwell's daughter got killed in—about six months ago. On the Merritt somewhere. And you might nudge Barney a little about the check out on Elwell's records." He paused. "Don't I know he'd rather we did," Bill said. "Good night, Mullins."

He turned back. Dorian looked at him. "I remembered," he told her. "Detectives have to sleep."

"I think," Pam said, "somebody's hinting. We'll—"

But they loitered with intent.

"Just that Elwell's brother would rather wait until morning to tell us he knows nothing about this 'shocking business,' " Bill said. "And—preliminary findings on the autopsy." He paused, seemed to consider. "Probably won't get us anywhere," Bill said. "Except give us another thing to check on. Elwell wouldn't have lived more than six months or a year. Even, the M.E. thinks, with an operation."

Pam said, "Oh," and there was shock in her voice. "Did—did he know?"

Bill shrugged. Whether Jameson Elwell had known how much his life drew in was something they, perhaps, would never know. They would try to find a doctor he might have gone to, who might have told him.

"But," Bill said, "the M.E. says there needn't have been any symptoms yet. So, unless he was in the habit of having regular checkups—and pretty thorough ones at that—" He ended with a shrug.

It was odd, Pam thought, that this somehow should make it worse, since Jamey was dead in any case—dead, it could be assumed, far more quickly, with a sudden flare of pain instead of pain endlessly smoldering. But—it did. Unfairness added to unfairness, in some fashion not altogether clear. Dear Jamey—

Jerry was closing the door behind him when Pam North said, "Wait a minute," and turned back.

"Bill," she said. "There was a tape recorder in the laboratory. Was there anything on the tape?"

"No," Bill said. "There wasn't anything on the tape, Pam. As Mullins said—we don't get the easy ones."

4

From the other bed there were small sounds—sounds chiefly of rustling. There were also certain sighing sounds, and a small—obviously smothered—cough. Jerry North lengthened his breathing, approximated a mild snore. There was, from the other bed, the slight sound of someone turning over. This was followed by a somewhat louder sign. Jerry, under the covers, looked at the illuminated dial of his wrist watch. It showed twenty minutes of three.

"Oh, dear," Pam North said, in the soft voice of one who, driven almost beyond endurance, is still considerate of those more fortunate, those who can sleep. There were further sounds. Pam had, evidently, turned over on the other side. There was a swishing sound. Pam had, undoubtedly, thrown off excess covering. There was silence for a few minutes, but Jerry did not sleep. Jerry waited. There was a louder sigh, and a longer sigh. There was a small sound of creaking. Pam

was sitting up in bed, preparatory—it must be assumed—to pulling the covers back again.

"All right, Pam," Jerry said, and sat up in his own
bed, and turned on the light between their beds. At
which Pam said, "Ouch!" and covered her eyes. "I
tried not to wake you up," Pam said and turned to look
at him. He said nothing. "All right," she said. "I tried
to wake you up. Inadvertently."

"I know," Jerry said. "It's all right. I'll—"

"*Jerry!*" Pam said. "Of all the—*no.*" Jerry put his
legs back in bed. "Anyway, not yet," Pam said.

Jerry shook a cigarette loose from a package on the
night table and held it out to Pam, who took it. He
lighted hers, lighted one for himself.

"All right," he said. "I don't know who killed
Jamey. And I feel the same way about it you do.
And—I'm as wide awake now as you are. And—
you've thought of something. At"—he consulted his
watch again—"fifteen minutes of three."

"I can't help that," Pam said. "And probably it's all
wrong. But—this posthypnotic whatever it is."

"Oh, lord," Jerry said. "Suggestion. You want to
read the book?"

"Why should I?" Pam said. "It's a very long book.
And you've read it. Division of labor, sort of. That
sharing which is part of every true—"

"Pam!"

"—except that some people can sleep through anything." Pam said.

For a moment Jerry had the uneasy feeling that he
had carried things too far. He looked at Pam. She
wasn't cross. Intent, but not cross.

"Whatever I knowest, thou shalt know," Jerry said.

"Or we'll get the book and read it aloud to each other."

"All right," Pam said. "You can get somebody to break a clock. Could you get somebody to—kill?"

"You," Jerry said, "think of the damnedest things. At three o'clock in the morning. No, according to Elwell, and he says that that's the consensus."

"Are they sure?"

"Of course they—" Jerry said, and stopped. "Well—" he said.

They were sure enough, and a long series of experiments had been made—including several by Elwell himself. But there was one flaw in all the experiments. They weren't real—couldn't, obviously, be real. The only real experiment would involve real murder, which would be carrying things rather far. So they had tried to duplicate reality without actually achieving it. They had tried it with rubber daggers—but rubber daggers would hardly feel real to anyone, let alone to a person in hypnosis when, many think, perceptions are heightened. They had tried it with real daggers, but the "victim" behind a barrier of "invisible" glass. But— was the glass really invisible? They had tried it with guns loaded with blanks. But—did the operator unconsciously reveal to the subject that the gun held only blanks?

Under these simulated conditions, some subjects apparently tried to kill. Most authorities doubted that, with actual killing possible, any subject would murder—unless, presumably, he had murder already in his mind.

"So?"

"Suppose," Pam said, "this Mr. Hunter, under posthypnotic suggestion, broke a valuable clock because Jamey had told him the clock wasn't any longer valuable. Was worthless."

"All right," Jerry said. "Supposed."

"Suppose Jamey did know that he—he was going to die. That he—he wasn't any longer valuable. To himself. That for somebody to kill him would be—what's the long word?"

"Euthanasia. No, I doubt it, Pam. And—it would have been a dirty trick. Jamey didn't play dirty tricks."

"Oh," Pam said, "he'd leave a record of some sort, exonerating whoever did it. Because—that would be the point, wouldn't it? Of the final experiment? To prove that, under certain circumstances—very special circumstances—a person who had been hypnotized could be told to kill?"

Jerry doubted several things—one, that any explanation Jamey might leave behind would, legally, exonerate the person who killed him. Two—that anyone, most of all Jameson Elwell, would think the point important enough for so drastic a proof. Three—that it would have worked anyway.

" 'Hold then my sword and turn away thy face,
    'While I do run upon it. Wilt thou, Strato?'
and Strato did, as I remember it."

"But before that somebody—I forget who—had said, 'Not on your life.' Said—wait a minute—'That's not an office for a friend, my lord.' " Jerry spoke with some triumph.

"It could be," Pam said, "that Strato was the better friend, my lord. My God—I'm beginning to talk like Shakespeare."

Blank verse, Jerry told her, is infectious. It happens even to writers of prose—unwary writers of prose.

"All right, Pam said. "What I said can still be true. And—the more somebody loved Jamey, the more likely he would be to—to do what Jamey wanted. Save him from—from long pain. Pain without hope."

"I doubt—" Jerry said, and stopped. "All right," he said. "I still don't believe it. I'll admit—" He stopped again. "Damn," Jerry said, in a tone aggrieved. "He would have left a statement," he said.

"Of course. In his files. Or—*Jerry*. Perhaps he made it orally—on the tape recorder and—and *somebody wiped it off!* Or whatever you do to a tape."

"You can," Jerry said, "think of the damnedest things." He said if not without admiration. He ground out his cigarette and at once lighted a fresh one, having, it occurred to him, thought of a damnedest thing himself.

"Suppose this," he said. "Suppose somebody— anybody you like; this man Hunter for example— killed Elwell, just in the ordinary course of events. And—"

"*Jerry!*" Pam said. "The *ordinary* course—"

"Ssh," Jerry said. "You've had *your* supposes. This man doesn't want to be caught. But—suppose he is. With overpowering evidence against him. He says it certainly looks bad but he doesn't remember anything about it. And then—'If I did it, it was because he'd hypnotized me and made me do it, and I can prove that he did hypnotize me often and once made me break a clock.' I don't know whether it would get him off entirely, but if he could make it stick it would be— well, an extenuating circumstance, at the least."

He looked at Pam, who nodded, who said, "That's a very good suppose, dear," but seemed to be thinking of something else—something that smudged the clarity of her mobile face. He waited.

"Faith Oldham loved him," Pam said, slowly. "We both felt that—as a girl might love a father. A very good father—a wise father. I think she might have done almost anything he asked, feeling he knew best. And—I wonder if he ever hypnotized her, Jerry? And if—"

Her clear voice faltered a little.

"I hope it isn't that way," Pam North said. "Will you get me a phenobarbital, Jerry?"

Bill Weigand got to his office at a little before nine Thursday morning. Sergeant Mullins had been there earlier; Sergeant Mullins had been active, on two fronts.

Precinct detectives, who had been active even earlier, had got the name of a doctor from Professor Elwell's address book. Mullins, by telephone, had run the doctor to earth—specifically, to his hospital rounds. Yes, he had been consulted by Professor Elwell from time to time, over a period of years. If they wanted more than that—how did the doctor know Mullins was who he said he was? If he was, didn't the police know that doctors do not talk about patients?

Mullins himself was patient, tactful. Professor Elwell was dead. So the point of secrecy was hardly relevant. He had been shot to death, so the previous condition of his health had nothing to do with the end of his life. So—

"Doctors are stuffy," Mullins told Bill Weigand. "Wasted ten minutes getting around to it. No, he didn't know Elwell had anything seriously wrong with him. Matter of fact, he hadn't seen Elwell for some three years and then it was about nothing much, and Elwell seemed O.K."

"What was it then?"

Not that it mattered.

"Cat bit him," Mullins said. "You fool around with cats—Minor infection. Doc treated it."

It didn't matter.

"People ought to leave cats alone," Mullins said. "Speaking of which—did you know Jerry North published the professor's last book?"

"Yes," Bill said and to that, after a considerable pause, Mullins said, "Oh," in a certain way. "Not," he added, "that they're not nice people, Loot. Only—"

"This doctor wouldn't know whether Elwell had been to see another man?"

"No. I asked him. He said he doubted it, but it was up to anybody what doctor he went to."

Mullins had read from the preliminary autopsy report—read words over which he had stumbled slightly. Would Elwell necessarily have known that he was ill, or how ill he was? Not necessarily; in fact, probably not. In another few months—

"The accident?"

"Somebody," Mullins said, "ought to do something about the Merritt Parkway."

It was a statement with which Bill Weigand did not disagree. But it was not clear that, in the violent death of Elizabeth Elwell, twenty-four years and two months old when her life ended during the early morning of April twenty-sixth, the inadequacies of the Merritt had been much involved.

A Jaguar, being driven toward New York at around eighty, had gone out of control, crossed the center strip, crashed into a sedan headed east. A man and a woman, driving home to Norwalk after the theater in New York, and an after-theater supper, had been killed in the sedan. Elizabeth Elwell had been killed in the Jaguar—more exactly, had been killed as she was thrown from it to unrelenting pavement. Her fiancé, one Rosco Finch, in the Jaguar beside her, had been only slightly injured.

Finch and the girl had been driving back to New York after a party in Westport.

"Finch drunk?"

"It doesn't matter," Mullins said. "Finch wasn't driving. The girl was driving. She had a few drinks but not enough to make her drunk. If she had normal resistance. Concentration in the blood"—Mullins consulted notes—"a little less than a tenth of a per cent. Just lost control."

It had not been on a curve, but on a straightaway. It had, however, happened just as the Jaguar came over the top of a Merritt Parkway hill. Something might, of course, have showed up ahead—a car moving slowly in the fast lane, for example. The Jaguar's brakes had gone on just before it left the pavement and ploughed into the grass of the center strip. Finch didn't remember seeing anything, but he wasn't watching the road with much attention. In fact, he thought he had been dozing.

"Her car?"

It had been Finch's car.

"But she was driving?"

"That's what he says." Mullins looked at Bill Weigand and raised his eyebrows.

"Nothing," Bill said. "Oh, it's usually the passenger who gets thrown out. But not always."

"He was, apparently," Mullins said. "First. Landed on the grass. It was soft, the way it is in spring. You think it ties in?"

It didn't seem to.

They drove from Twentieth Street north to Forty-fourth, and across to the Harvard Club. Mr. Foster Elwell was waiting for them in the lounge. The lounge had an unawakened air.

Foster Elwell was a big man; an athlete who had softened with the years. There had, obviously, been a good many years—at a guess, Foster Elwell was several years older than his brother had been. He had a ruddy face and, probably, a blood pressure. He got out of a deep chair with the quickness of a man who rejected physical defeat. (Which conceivably, Bill thought, was not too good for him.)

He looked from Bill to Mullins and back to Bill, and his eyes questioned.

"No," Bill said. "We don't know yet, Mr. Elwell."

"It's a knockout," Foster Elwell said. "I don't mind telling you it's a knockout. A thing like this. To happen to Jamey." He shook his head. *"Jamey,"* he repeated. "Of all the people in the world."

Which was almost always said; which was almost always poignant, as it was now. Somebody else—somebody far away—somebody read about in the newspapers. Such distant things could be believed.

"Any way I can help. Any damn way at all," Foster Elwell said. "Get my hands on the son of a bitch who'd do a thing like that."

"We'll get him," Bill promised, and hoped they would. They almost always did. Of course, there had been another Elwell and they hadn't. Which was a coincidence without meaning. Which had better be.

"I'll do anything I can," Foster Elwell said. "I don't know what it'll be. My brother and I—we were close enough, but we didn't see each other a lot. Know what I mean? Once a month, maybe—once every six weeks. Last time was—" He thought. "Labor Day," he said. "He came out to the place."

He knew of no enemies his brother might have had, of no circumstance in his brother's life which might have led to this. Everybody liked Jamey; he couldn't imagine anybody not liking Jamey. And the things Jamey did for people—

"Right now," he said, "my son Jimmy's in college because—" He stopped, as if he had started something he preferred not to finish. "All right," he said, "I'm retired. We've got just about enough to live on decently. I don't say we wouldn't have put Jimmy—he's our youngest—through college somehow, but all the same— And he helped with Janet. She's married now. Fine young man but they're out in Scranton and—"

He stopped.

"Getting along," he said. "Have to expect it, I suppose. Fact is, this whole thing's got me—fuzzy. Having a cocktail, Grace and I were, just like any evening and the telephone rings and—I tell you, captain, it's a knockout. I know I sound like a meandering old fool. But—"

It was natural, Bill said, and that Elwell was not meandering. And what Elwell said about his brother echoed what everybody said.

"He must," Bill said, "have been a fine man."

"The best."

"He had a good deal of money?"

"Yes. Funny thing, isn't it? Here he was, a professor—supposed not to know about things like that. And here I am—or was—a broker. Supposed to know a lot. And he starts with his part of what dad left us and everything he invested in—wow! And I start with the same amount and—well, there you are. Doesn't make much sense, but there you are."

"Do you happen to know how he left his money? We'll check up on that, of course, but if you happen to know?"

"Yes," Elwell said. "Told me that last time I saw him. Split four ways—my kids, there's Foster and Jimmy and Janet, and this daughter of his old friend. Girl named—" He hesitated.

"Faith Oldham?"

"That's it. Faith Oldham. All to the younger generation. A great believer in the younger generation. Always doing something to help kids. And now some son of a bitch—"

It was evident, then, that something had occurred to the big man.

"Hey," he said, and leaned forward in his chair. "What the hell're you getting at? About how he left his money? Sounds to me as if you—"

Bill shook his head.

"Not getting at anything," Bill said. "One of the things we always have to find out about. You can understand that, Mr. Elwell. A routine thing."

"Better be," Elwell said, but then leaned back. "Sure," he said. "I realize you have to ask about it."

About those who stand to profit, directly or indirectly. It was as good a time as any other, and Foster Elwell wouldn't like it. Foster Elwell didn't like it;

68

said, "Now what the hell business is that—" and stopped. He said, O.K., he hadn't spent all the previous day in Westport. He had driven in to New York to have lunch with a friend—"on business, I've still got a little business"—and back after lunch. He had lunched in midtown; he was not sure what time he had started to drive back, but it must have been around three, because he had got home between four-thirty and five. It had been about five-thirty, or a little later, that the telephone had rung, and it had been the city police to tell him. And if Weigand wanted to check up on him, he could ask the man he had lunched with and the man was—

Mullins jotted down the name of the man, as he had jotted down a number of things.

"Mr. Elwell," Bill said, "did you know your brother was a sick man? A very sich man?"

Elwell shook his head. He said, "How sick?"

"He would have lived six months," Bill said. "Perhaps a year."

Elwell said, "Jesus," and then, "What a lousy break." And then, "I suppose it showed up in the autopsy?"

"Right," Bill said. "You didn't know about it? He never said anything about it?"

"No," Foster Elwell said, and spoke in a dull voice. "Last time I saw him, he looked fine. Said he felt fine. And all the time—" He shook his head and there was uneasiness in his face, the shadow of fear. You get along and it comes closer; each new example brings it closer still.

"Did he know about it?" Foster said, and Bill Weigand said that Professor Elwell might have known and might not have known; that the assistant medical examiner said there might, as yet, have been no symptoms.

"Maybe he was lucky," Elwell said. "Maybe it was a break, in a way. But—it hasn't anything to do with what happened, has it?"

"Not that I can see," Bill said. "Except the obvious—if whoever killed him had known how short a time he had to live the killer might have waited. But that's only a guess, of course."

The big man nodded slowly, as one does to note the obvious. There was a considerable pause and, since Bill thought Foster Elwell might be about to speak, Bill did not break it.

"Look," Elwell said, "I said that as far as I knew everybody liked Jamey. That I couldn't imagine anyone not liking him."

"Yes," Bill said.

"There's one man who maybe didn't like him much," Elwell said. "You know about Liz?"

"His daughter? Yes. Elizabeth."

"Elizabeth," Elwell said. "Everybody called her Liz. My time they'd have called her Beth, maybe Betty. Nobody thought Liz was pretty enough. Shows how we—" He brought himself back; shook his head dolefully at this new evidence of his tendency to meander. "This man she was going to marry," he said. "Rosco Finch. Hell of a name, ain't it? Says he wasn't driving when it happened. Jamey thought he was. Matter of fact, Jamey's been trying to prove he was. Hired some detective fellows."

Bill said that that was interesting—damn interesting. And what had made Jameson Elwell think that?

"Maybe," Jameson Elwell's brother said, "mostly because he wanted to. He realized that himself. On the other hand, there are tricks about driving a Jag. Person who's used to—oh, say a Buick. A Cadillac—has to learn the tricks. As far as Jamey knew, Liz hadn't learned them."

"But," Bill said, "would he know?"

There was that. Jameson Elwell had realized there was that. On the other hand, he and his daughter had been good friends; usually, when something new interested her, she talked about it to him. And, she was interested in cars. And—she hadn't talked about Jaguars.

It was, certainly, anything but conclusive. Foster Elwell realized that; his brother had realized that.

"Mostly, I guess," Foster Elwell said, "it was just a hunch of Jamey's. Partly because he didn't want to think his daughter had killed two people, and herself, by being—irresponsible. But there was more than that—I'll give Jamey that, and that he knew about the way minds work. His job, you know."

Bill knew. He said, "Yes."

"Ordinary person," Elwell said, "tells you somebody else is a certain kind of person, and you say to yourself, 'That's just what he thinks.' Know what I mean? Jamey said it and, damn it all, you believed him. At the bottom, I suppose, he was just sure that his daughter wouldn't drink too much if she was going to drive, and wouldn't drive too fast for conditions and wouldn't lose her nerve. Tell you how he put it. He said she was 'emotionally' a good driver. And that drivers like that don't go over the top of a hill at eighty, particularly at night."

"Miss Elwell hadn't been drinking," Bill said. "At least, she had been, but not enough to matter. Unless she was particularly susceptible."

"Not Liz," Elwell said. "Show me one of them is, nowadays. I don't say she ever drank much. But now and then—hell, now and then everybody has a few, if they're normal. Liz never showed anything. Know what I mean?"

"Yes," Bill said. "But—it isn't much to go on, Mr. Elwell. Your brother was fond of his daughter, probably. Didn't like having to remember—well, that she was irresponsible. Had killed a couple of innocent people."

"Sure," Elwell said. "I said that. Also—he realized that himself. Wasn't much he didn't realize. Of course—the car was this fellow Finch's. Mostly a man owns one of those jobs, he likes to drive it himself. Why he owns it, as much as anything. Also, he was driving when they left that evening, Jamey said. He looked down from upstairs and watched them drive off, and Finch was driving. Doesn't prove anything about who drove later on. I'll give you that. Look—I don't suppose there's anything to this. Only—put Finch on the spot a bit if Jamey was right, and could prove it. Wouldn't it? Lose his license, for one thing."

"More than that," Bill said. "Possibly more than that, anyway. Might be vehicular homicide, if it looked bad enough. Did Finch know your brother was having the thing investigated?"

"Hell," Elwell said, "*I* don't know, captain. If these detective fellows went around to Finch and began asking him questions, he'd know somebody was interested. Maybe they'd tell you who. I don't know. Maybe—you say it might be homicide?"

"Vehicular," Bill said. "Yes, they might be that rough on him. And certainly he would lose his driver's license for a long time. You happen to know what he

72

does for a living? I mean, if he's a salesman, travels by car—"

"He's a golf pro," Elwell said. "Fairly big time. Don't you play golf, captain?"

"No."

"If you did, you'd have heard of Finch," Elwell told him. "Tournament player. Won quite a few. I suppose he drives from tournament to tournament. Most of them do. Be a bit of a problem if he couldn't use a car, I suppose. So if he thought Jamey—but hell, you get what I'm driving at. Long way ahead of me, probably."

Bill was at least up with him. It was tenuous. It was also interesting. Did Elwell know what firm of private detectives his brother had employed?

Elwell didn't. Elwell had, Bill thought, told them all he did know—this subject to a detective's reservations. ("A good detective is always more or less suspicious and very inquisitive."—*Manual of Procedure, Police Department of the City of New York.*) Bill thanked Foster Elwell for his help, repeated expressions of sympathy, said they would get in touch with him if it appeared he might help further; left him in the lounge and went to a telephone booth. Mullins stood outside the partly open door of the booth.

Would precinct send a man to ask—Bill reached for Mullins's proffered notebook and read a name from it—if he had lunched with Foster Elwell the day before, and, if he had, at what time he and Elwell had parted? And, how far had they got through the papers in Jameson Elwell's office? Through, for example, his recent checkbooks?

They had. Was anything of interest? Did the name of any payee jump at them?

73

A few. Checks to Hunter, for example. Checks to one James Elwell. In both cases, these seemed to represent regular modest payments. "Like they were working for him," the precinct man said. And one other payee had aroused some interest—Investigators, Inc. Bill knew? Pretty good size agency; supposed to be pretty much on the up and up.

Bill knew. The offices of Investigators, Inc., were in midtown. They might, Bill told Mullins, as well stop by there on their way elsewhere. "Sure," Mullins said, "only if there was anything like that the State cops would of tumbled to it." He paused. "You'd think," he added. He considered further. "Only it would be sorta hard to check out," he said.

Miles Flanagan of Investigators, Inc., said they would be glad to do anything they could that would help the police, as weren't they always? As for example?

Bill gave him the example.

Flanagan pulled his lower lip over his upper, indicating judicial contemplation. He said, yes, he had read about the professor. He said that under the circumstances, without prejudice, because normally they didn't give the names of clients—

"Come off it," Bill Weigand said and Flanagan looked a little hurt, and said he was getting to it as fast as he could. But he did get there faster.

Professor Jameson Elwell had employed them to find out what they could about the accident—specifically, to unearth any evidence they could that Finch, not the girl, had been driving.

"Look," Flanagan said, although Weigand had said nothing, "I told him it was cold—this was three-four months after it happened—and why had he waited so long? He said he realized it was late, and that I had an interesting psychological point about his delay—and I'll be damned if he didn't sound as if the point *did* interest him. I said we couldn't promise anything, and he said he realized that. I said the chances were he was just throwing his money away—"

"I'm sure you were highly ethical," Bill Weigand said. "So—you took the case. And, as you expected, it was cold and you didn't get anything. Right?"

"For God's sake, captain," Flanagan said. "You're in the business. You know how the cookie crumbles. If you think we didn't work on it—but hell. The girl dead. The people they ran into dead. Nobody at the party they'd been at could remember which of them was driving. The girl got thrown out, but so did Finch."

"You didn't get anything?"

"Nothing to pin anything on. Finch had been drinking a good bit. The girl hadn't. He thought pretty well of himself as a driver and he hadn't had the Jag long. Sort of a new toy, which makes you wonder. But he says—"

"You did go to him?"

"Look," Flanagan said. "I told you we worked on it. The professor didn't say anything about not going to Finch. Sure we went to him."

"As insurance investigators, I suppose?"

"Well—" Flanagan said. "It could be he thought that. Only—the insurance boys had already been around. Nothing we could do about that. So, it could be he thought somebody else was nosing around about it. Since he seems to be a pretty bright boy. You play golf, captain?"

"No."

75

"Ought to. It's a great game."

"I'm sure," Bill said. "He said it was the girl driving, of course?"

"Sure. Said just before they started out he decided maybe he'd had one more than he needed and asked her if she'd take over. If you drink, don't drive. All very—law abiding. Says he was half asleep when it happened and doesn't know how it happened, except maybe she dozed off too. Says she was a good driver, but not used to a Jag, and maybe that was it. Says he plain doesn't know. Acts all broken up about it. I'll give him that."

"Or—scared?"

Flanagan pulled his lower lip again over his upper lip.

"Have it your own way, captain," he said. "Oh—I read you. Have it your own way."

"You reported this to the professor?"

"Sure—he was paying us. I said we were sorry and advised him not to waste any more money. Told him I didn't think we'd ever get anything that would stand up. And—"

He paused.

"That's all," he said.

"Except one thing," Bill said. "You were on this yourself?" Flanagan nodded. "You've been around," Bill said. "What did you think yourself?"

"Off the record?"

"Off the record."

"Because I wouldn't want to slander anybody."

"Because you wouldn't want to slander anybody."

"O.K.," Flanagan said. "I think he was lying like hell, captain. I think he was driving and had had one too many and—well, could be he dozed off. And when he found out the girl was dead and he wasn't, and that nothing could hurt her more than she was hurt—well. You can see what he might have done, can't you?"

"Yes," Bill said.

"Without liking it," Flanagan said. "I don't say it makes him the All-American boy."

"No," Bill said. "You didn't tell him who was hiring you?" Flanagan looked hurt, and shook his head. "But he might have guessed?"

"Now how the hell would I know about that?" Flanagan said. He looked at Bill Weigand. He had surprisingly shrewd eyes. "I said he seems pretty bright," Flanagan said. "Quite a bright boy, I'd say he is." He paused again. "Might annoy him, mightn't it?" he said. "Having his word doubted and all that?"

5

Sergeant Mullins would seek out Rosco Finch and ask him whether he had killed Professor Elwell because it annoyed him to have his word doubted—and because the professor might have got him put in jail, which would have interfered with his golf. "Man would get rusty in five-ten years," Mullins pointed out. "And seems like that's the way he makes his living."

Bill agreed a man might get very rusty in five-ten years; perhaps so rusty he might have to find other employment.

"Funny name," Mullins said and then, "I used to play it when I was a kid."

Bill had been about to start the Buick's engine. He took his foot off the accelerator.

"Golf?" he said. It seemed, somehow, a little unlike Mullins, but one could never tell.

"Hell no, Loot," Mullins said. "Me and golf? Finch."

"Finch?"

"Sure. Card game. A lot of kids play it. Did anyway when I was a kid."

Bill Weigand seined his mind. Something darted through it, slippery and elusive. Something of no conceivable importance, and for that reason the more annoying.

Finch? Rosco Finch? A game named Finch? Not, surely, a game named Rosco. Mullins had said—

"Flinch!" Bill said, the slippery fish netted. "That's what you played, sergeant."

"In Brooklyn," Mullins said, and spoke with dignity. "In Brooklyn it was finch."

Mullins lifted the hand of authority, and a cab stopped. His hand on the door handle, Mullins relented.

"In Manhattan," he said, "it could have been flinch." He got into the cab.

Bill Weigand drove uptown. He parked on the sloping street in front of the two houses of the late Jameson Elwell. He went down the two steps from sidewalk to the front door of the house Faith Oldham lived in with her mother. A small sign beside the door said "No Peddlers." He rang the bell and, after some time, the door opened.

It was opened by a slight woman in a print dress, who at first seemed to be a very young woman and then, in almost the same moment of observation, did not. She was a woman in, at a guess, her late fifties; perhaps even in her sixties. She had very brown hair— too brown hair. A dye job by some beauty shop around the corner, Bill guessed; not a job one of the big shops would have countenanced. The print dress too youthful, although there was nothing the matter with the figure it covered. The eyes, which he looked down into—since they looked frostily up at him—were blue, coldly blue.

"Can't you read, young man?" the young-old woman asked him. Her voice was a little thin. She pointed at the enameled sign which said "No Peddlers."

"I'm not selling anything, Mrs. Oldham," Bill said, thinking he took no chance. The blueness of eyes was the same. But there was no coldness in Faith Oldham's eyes. Not, certainly, when she thought of "Uncle Jamey." Not, for that matter, when she looked at Carl Hunter.

"I'm a police officer, Mrs. Oldham," Bill said. "Investigating Professor Elwell's death. I wonder if you could give me a few minutes? You and your daughter, if she's here?"

"At school," Mrs. Hope Oldham said. "But there's nothing we can tell you."

"Probably not," Bill said. "My name's Weigand, by the way. Captain Weigand. We have to ask a lot of useless questions, I'm afraid."

"I don't see—" Mrs. Oldham said, but then, "All right, come in if you have to. But it can't be too long, because I was just going out."

She led him up a flight of stairs, opened a door and went into a living room at the front of the house. She sat down in a chair by one of the two tall windows—a chair from which she could look out the window. Something in her movements made Weigand believe that the chair she had gone to was "her" chair; that she sat in it a good deal, and looked out the window a good deal.

"All right," she said. "What do you want to know,

captain? That you think I or my daughter could tell you?"

It was possible, Bill told her, and sat down to face her, although without invitation—it was possible that Professor Elwell's assailant could have come through this house, gained access from it to the laboratory on the top floor, gone from there to the office. It was not certain; they had to check everything.

"Through a locked door?" Mrs. Oldham said.

There are keys to unlock doors. She had one to the front door; so, presumably, did her daughter. Her daughter had a key also to the laboratory.

He saw new frost in the blue eyes. He kept talking. Keys sometimes get misplaced; it is a matter of minutes only to cut new keys with the old available; almost any hardware store can do it in minutes.

"Oh," she said. "Well, I'm sure I've never misplaced, as you put it, my door key. As to the door upstairs, I wasn't honored. Not I. You'll have to ask Faith about that. And she isn't here."

"Assuming somebody had the necessary keys," Bill said, "could he come through the house without you or your daughter hearing him, or seeing him?"

That was, she told him, a foolish question. It depended on where she and her daughter were in the house, or whether they were in it at all. If they were in one of the rear rooms, say, with the doors closed—of course someone could go up, and come down for that matter, unseen and unheard.

"But if you mean yesterday," Mrs. Oldham said, "and I suppose you do—neither of us was here when it happened. *If* it happened the way you told my daughter. She went off somewhere at a little before three and I went a few minutes later. *And* locked the door. Went out to do the errands. *She* never has time for errands."

Bill nodded his head. He said he had supposed that to be the way of it, since neither of them had heard the shot, which they could hardly have helped doing if they were in the house.

"Well," she said, "as to that. The laboratory—what he called the laboratory, and I don't know why, I'm sure—is soundproofed. Anyway, that's what Faith tells me. So how can you be sure we'd have heard the shot, especially in the other house?"

That was very true, Bill told her, in a tone which complimented. They would have to make some tests. (He supposed that, eventually, they would. But Elwell had been shot while he sat close to a window. Sound passes readily through window glass.)

On another subject—he had heard that Elwell and her late husband had been great friends. Presumably, then, she had herself known Elwell at least fairly well. Could she—

"You see, Mrs. Oldham," Bill said, "one of the things we try to do is to find out everything we can about the victim in a case like this. Sometimes very small things prove significant."

"My late husband," Mrs. Oldham said, "thought Elwell was a great friend of his. Thought so until the day he died, the poor, trusting man."

Which was entirely unexpected. Bill let surprise show on his face.

"Oh," she said, "I know what they've been telling you. Don't think I don't. Maybe a lot of people were taken in. Maybe they wanted to be, too. A man makes a lot of money, *however* he makes it, and you'll find plenty of people to say what a great man he is."

"That's true, of course," Bill Weigand said. "But

everybody I've talked to so far seems to have had—" he hesitated momentarily—"very high regard for Professor Elwell."

"I don't doubt it," she said. *"People!"* Her tone dismissed "people." "I suppose you've heard what a kind, generous man he was to let the widow and daughter of his dear old friend live in this house. Without paying rent?"

"Well—"

"Of course you have. Even my own daughter says things like that. Believes them, for all I know. If it was anything, it was conscience. C-o-n-s-c-i-e-n-c-e. Only, maybe it was something else."

"Conscience?"

"A lot of people could tell you," she said. "Oh—I suppose they won't. Let sleeping dogs lie. Don't bring up unpleasant things, especially about such a good, kind man who has so much money. However he made it."

"I understood," Bill said, "that he made it in the stock market."

"Of course he did," Mrs. Oldham said. "Have you got a cigarette, young man?" He had; he gave her a cigarette, and lighted it. "And based everything he did on theories my late husband worked out. Did you think Jameson Elwell was bright enough to do it on his own?"

"Well," Bill said. "Yes, I did, Mrs. Oldham."

"You see?" she said. "Even now—the—the *image*. My late husband often used the word about Professor Elwell."

"Did he? And these theories—about stock market trends, I suppose. Your husband was interested in that sort of thing?"

"As a hobby," she said. "An intellectual exercise. Child's play to a mind like his—a truly great mind."

"But I gather," Bill said, "that he didn't himself play the market. That is—"

"Make money out of it, you mean?" she said. "Certainly not. He considered it merely a form of gambling, of course. Was perfectly content to see his old friend"—there was a certain inflection on the word "friend," as there had been earlier—"make whatever he could by stealing somebody else's ideas. Of course that was before—but I suppose you're one of those speak-no-ill-of-the-dead people?"

"I could hardly be," Bill said. "Not in my trade, Mrs. Oldham. Before what?"

"All right," she said. "This kind, wonderful Professor Elwell of yours didn't stop with that. That my late husband wouldn't have minded. Ideas—that was different. Captain—*half the ideas in Professor Elwell's books were stolen*—yes, *stolen*—from my late husband. And—everybody knows it, captain. You just make them admit it. That's all you have to do."

"You do," he said, "put the professor in quite a different light, Mrs. Oldham."

"High time somebody did," she said.

"Your daughter didn't feel this way."

"My daughter," she said. "The poor innocent child. Just a child, captain—a trusting child. But thank heaven Arnold will be around to protect her when I'm gone."

It occurred to Bill Weigand that he had seldom seen a person who looked less on the verge of going. He did not mention this. He said, "Arnold?"

"Arnold Ames," she said. "The man she's going to

marry, of course. One of *the* Ameses, fortunately. And such a dear boy."

"Ames?" Bill repeated. "I thought she and young Hunter—"

"Carl Hunter?" she said. "What ever put that idea in your head? Oh—she sees him now and then, of course. And she's sorry for him, probably. But as for anything more—*really,* captain."

Bill said he must have been wrong.

"About a good many things, I wouldn't wonder," she said.

"It looks that way," he said. "I must say your daughter—"

"Oh," she said, "Jameson Elwell could fool people—particularly young, inexperienced people. I told you that just now. Softsoaping—that's what they call it nowadays, I understand."

She had given him a good deal to think about, Bill told her, standing up. A good deal to look into. He had merely hoped to find out if, in the house, the "coast had been clear" the day before. It was interesting to find out it had, with both her and her daughter out. He had found out so much more.

"I suppose," she said, "I did straighten you out about some things. Just remember—a lot of people know what the professor was really like. You'll find out if you ask them."

Bill said he would ask them. He said he could find his own way out. He paused at the door and turned back.

"By the way," he said. "One thing I almost forgot. Was your daughter ever hypnotized by Professor Elwell?"

She looked at him in apparent astonishment.

"Never!" she said. "Hypnotism! I wouldn't have permitted it. Not in a thousand years. That awful, *evil,* business!"

He thanked her again and went out and closed the door behind him. It was a heavy door; the house belonged to an era when men built heavily. Rooms on this floor, and on the ground floor, could be closed off from the stair hall by four such heavy doors, and probably usually were. So—anyone who took the trouble to walk quietly could climb two flights of stairs and nobody the wiser, whether anybody was in the house or not.

Bill climbed the second flight and used the key he had taken from Faith Oldham and let himself into the laboratory. It was empty. He crossed the room, thinking about keys. Elwell would, of course, have had a key to the front door of the house the Oldhams lived in, since it was his house. If Elwell, then quite possibly his daughter. If his daughter, then quite possibly the man she had been going to marry, Rosco Finch. (Bill resisted the temptation to think of him as "Flinch.") It was worth bearing in mind, for what it was worth.

Bill went through the "closet" into the office, which was not empty. Two men, one at the desk and the other at the typewriter table, were going through papers. But of them looked at Weigand sharply, and relaxed, and he said, "Hi. Getting places?"

They looked at each other. "Nothing that sticks out much," the man at the desk said. "You want to—"

"Not now," Bill said.

He picked up the telephone on the desk and called his office. Mullins had located Rosco Finch at his apartment near Washington Square and made an appointment with him and gone to keep it. Mr. Gerald North had called, and wanted the captain to call back when he had the chance, but had added that it was nothing pressing. Deputy Chief Inspector Artemus O'Malley wanted to be filled in. "Reporters," Sergeant Stein, holding down the desk, reported succinctly.

"You didn't," Bill said, "happen to mention that Jerry North had called?"

"Good God no," Stein said. "You think I'd do a thing like that?"

"No," Bill said. "Anything else?"

"They threw the book at Puggy Wormser," Stein said. "Hit him with it, too."

"Good," Bill said, not really caring much. "I'm going up to Dyckman. Have another talk with a Professor Wahmsley, if he's free. Tell Arty we're being eager beavers."

He replaced the handpiece. He took it up again, drew a telephone number out of his mind, where he had filed it the day before, dialed it, asked for Professor Eugene Wahmsley, was asked politely to wait a moment, got "Miss Spencer speaking" and asked again for Wahmsley, heard "Surely" and then heard "Wahmsley," in a crisp voice.

"Sure," Professor Wahmsley said. "About half an hour'll do O.K., captain."

Sergeant Aloysius Mullins was sorry he couldn't tell Rosco Finch what Investigators, Inc., was supposed to be up to.

"For all I know, Mr. Flinch," Mullins said. "They

haven't been up to anything. But we get this squeal—
this complaint. So they tell me, see what you can find
out. They're licensed, you know. We ride herd, in a
way of speaking."

"Finch, not Flinch."

"Sure," Mullins said. "They did send a man around
to see you about—it was about this accident last
spring, wasn't it, Mr. Flinch? None of our business,
and anyway that's all cleaned up. Hate to bring it up
again, Mr. Flinch."

"*Finch.* Yes. Anyway, a man who said his name was
Flanagan, said he worked for something called Investigators, Inc., came around. Asked a lot of fool questions about—about me and—Liz." He hesitated, Mullins noticed, on the girl's name. That was understandable enough. A man would.

"What we want to know," Mullins said, "did Flanagan pretend he was representing an insurance company? That's the sort of thing we don't like."

Mullins hoped Flinch wouldn't ask why they didn't
like it. Since "they" could hardly care less.

"Why?" Finch said. "Why do you people care one
way or the other?"

"Misrepresentation," Mullins said, giving each syllable the full treatment—tolling the word. Spoken so,
it sounded somewhat like a new type of felony.

"Oh," Finch said. "Yes, Flanagan did give me that
impression. I don't know that he actually said it
straight out."

"Slippery customers," Mullins said, with the air of a
man who hates slippery customers. "Wanted to know
if you were sure you weren't the one driving the car, I
shouldn't wonder."

"That was all settled a long time ago," Finch said.

"If you know anything about the accident, you know that."

"Sure," Mullins said. "We know it. The Connecticut police know it. Which makes us wonder—"

Rosco Finch was a tall, tanned man in his early thirties—a man with sun-bleached hair; a man with a well-ordered face and a somewhat small mouth. A good-looking man, all the same. So far as Mullins could determine, a man unperturbed. A late sleeper, apparently; he wore a robe over pajamas.

"—what these customers were up to," Mullins said. "You must have wondered yourself, Mr. Flinch. Or did you believe Flanagan was from the insurance company?"

"I do wish," Finch said, "you'd manage—" He shrugged, giving it up. "O.K." he said. "My insurance company, the insurance company these other people had—" He stopped. "I keep trying to forget it," Finch said. "The way—the way everything looked."

"Sure," Mullins said. "I know how you feel, Mr. Flinch. People had already been around from the insurance company so you couldn't help feeling it was a bit fishy?"

"Well," Finch said, "I guess I did. More after he'd gone than while he was here. You know how you begin to wonder about things?"

Mullins nodded his head.

"But," Finch said, "it didn't really matter a damn. I'd told it often enough and—there wasn't anything I was trying to hide. It was all in the papers, anyway. Liz was Professor Elwell's daughter—and well, people who follow golf—hell, you know how it is."

"Sure," Mullins said. "One of the things we're

trying to find out, Mr. Flinch—who were they representing? Or claim to be representing? We've checked back with both insurance companies and no soap."

"O.K.," Finch said. "I can't say I'm surprised. But—what were they up to then, sergeant?"

"What we're trying to find out," Mullins told him. "Figured you might—well, when you thought it over—might be able to come up with something'd give us a lead. You can't think of anybody'd be stirring things up again. Somebody with a grudge against you, maybe?"

"Grudge against me?"

"Just guessing," Mullins said. "Could be there'd be an angle there. Somebody trying to make out you were driving, when all the time it was the girl. Man like you, competing for these prizes. Quite big prizes, aren't they?"

"Some of them are," Finch said. "I don't get what you're driving at."

"Somebody you've beat out of a prize," Mullins said. "Or maybe would some time. I mean—you're pretty good at this golf, they tell me. Maybe somebody who ain't so good—did you think of that at all, Mr. Flinch?"

"That's preposterous," Finch said.

About which, Mullins thought, he's certainly right enough. Mullins managed, however, to look doubtful. He said, "Well—"

"I wouldn't waste time on that, sergeant."

Mullins said, "Well—" again; a man half convinced. He looked worried.

"All the same," he said, "people like Flanagan don't waste time unless there's money in it. Of course, there's the shakedown. Or, he could have thought there was. Get something on you—be able to make it look as if you had been driving the car. He might think you'd pay up to keep it quiet. Vehicular homicide and all. But then, he'd have been back, wouldn't he? And he wasn't?"

Mullins shook his head, a man bemused.

"There wasn't any suggestion of that," Finch said. "Listen—vehicular homicide?"

"Could be," Mullins said. "Connecticut's pretty tough, Mr. Flinch. You've got a New York license, I suppose. But still—"

"As a mater of fact," Finch said, "I've got a Connecticut license. Do some teaching at a club up there when I'm not on the circuit. But hell—*I wasn't driving.*"

"Sure you weren't," Mullins said. "That's what makes it so screwy. You haven't any notion what this customer Flanagan was after? Any at all?"

Finch shook his head. He said he was sorry he wasn't being more helpful—

"Hold it a minute," Mullins said. "Here's another angle—suppose somebody wanted to prove this girl— this Miss Elwell—*wasn't* driving. See what I mean? Clear her name. And maybe there'd be more to it than that. Some angle we don't know about."

Mullins's face lighted up a little to mirror this modest inspiration. It was the expression of someone who thinks that, for special acumen, he deserves a small pat on the head.

"You've got quite an imagination, sergeant," Finch said, in a tone which did not pat the waiting head. "Liz—Liz is dead. Nothing—nothing'll do her any good now. It's all written off."

Mullins's face showed acceptance, disappointed acceptance. He nodded his head to underline that. He said he guessed Mr. Flinch—"sorry, Finch. Can't think what's wrong with me this morning"—had something there. And, if anything came to Mr. Flinch, would he let them know? Sometimes things do come up that way—

"Sure," Finch said. "I don't imagine anything will."

To which Mullins sighed acceptance.

"Anyway," he said, "gets me out in the air, this kind of thing. Mostly they tie me down at a desk. And it's mighty nice weather for this time of year. Little cooler than yesterday. Must make you want to get out on the court, Mr. Finch."

"Course," Finch said. "Oh—I get out. Have to keep in practice. Spent all yesterday afternoon trying to get a few more yards into my drives. Up at this club in Connecticut."

"Must have been nice up there," Mullins said, although it is not easy for Mullins to believe that the country is ever "nice." "Weather like this probably brings a lot of golfers out at this club."

It was a little clumsy; it didn't, however, matter too much now.

"Not in midweek," Finch said. "Not this late in the season. Anyway, you don't practice driving with a lot of players on the fairway, sergeant. Had it mostly to myself yesterday afternoon. From lunch until pretty near dark."

Which covered that—and covered it pretty thinly.

Mullins left, then. Mr. Finch's morning newspaper was outside his apartment door, as it had been when Mullins arrived. This time, Sergeant Mullins picked it up. It was folded several times. One fold cut through a headline. What was visible read:

KMAN
ESSOR
SLAIN

Mullins said, "Oh, here's your paper," and handed it in, and Rosco Finch took it and said, "Thanks."

So—if Flinch didn't know already that Jameson Elwell had been shot to death, he would in a few minutes. *If* he didn't know already. And he would put two and two together, undoubtedly, since he seemed a bright enough young man.

Mullins called the office. Weigand wasn't in; Stein was still anchor man.

"Bill wants you to check out on young Hunter, Al," Stein said. "After that, meet him for lunch. He's gone up to Dyckman to talk to a professor named Wahmsley. Meet him for lunch at the Algonquin about one. Check?"

"Sure," Mullins said.

"With Mr. and Mrs. North," Stein said.

"Oh," Mullins said. "Does Arty know?"

"Not from me," Stein said. "We can hope and pray, Al."

6

Martini, sitting on the window sill, turned her head when Pam came into the bedroom and said, "Ouoowagh," accenting the last syllable. She also laid back her brown and pointed ears. She had been looking down at the sunny street, too far below, so her blue eyes were almost black.

"No," Pam said, "you can't go out, Teeney. Not until we go back to the country next spring. But I do think you're speaking much more clearly than you used to. 'Out,' Teeney. Say 'Ouoot.' Without the 'wagh.' "

"Mroough-a," Martini said, relapsing into her native Siamese. "Ow-*ah*."

"I don't know, I'm sure," Pam said. "There's no use being so gruff about it. You know you can't go out in New York, and there aren't any mice here anyway. I mean—there are probably a great many mice, but they aren't available. Nice Teeney."

Teeney closed her eyes, as if in thought, opened

94

them part way—partly opened they slanted sharply upward—and made a remark and waited.

"Duh baby," Pam North said. "Duh *pretty* baby."

Martini blinked again, slowly, basking in human speech, in affection. She did, however, look back over her shoulder at the window. She spoke briefly.

"I know," Pam said. "It's very limiting to be an apartment house cat again." Martini interrupted. "Cat," Pam repeated, because Martini likes to be reassured by direct address, and "cat" does as well, or almost as well, as "Teeney." "Particularly for a cat of your vigor. Duh baby. And who doesn't have the dissatisfaction of knowing how old she is. Which must be a pleasant way to be."

"Mrow-ow," Martini said, the last syllable added very quickly. She got off the window sill and came to Pam and rubbed against her legs, revolving around them, dark brown tail carried high.

"Goodness," Pam said. "I can't stand around talking to you all morning. Somebody's coming."

"Ur-agh," Martini said. Martini does not really like company, thinking more than two humans—and those carefully selected—make a crowd.

Pam sat at her dressing table and flicked her hair, and said, "No," firmly when Martini tried to get on her lap to help. Martini sat on the floor and stared at Pam as if she had never seen her before, and didn't like her much now. "And don't sulk," Pam said and powdered her nose and then, apropos of nothing in particular, stuck out her tongue at her reflection.

Half an hour, Faith Oldham had said, and it must now, at a quarter of eleven by a small wrist watch (which Pam was almost sure she had remembered to wind), be time for her to come. Under, presumably, a misapprehension with which both Pam and Jerry North are long familiar.

"We're not detectives," Pam would tell Faith Oldham. "We've never been detectives. All we do is *know* a detective."

She would be, as usual, listened to politely. At least, when they had met at Jameson Elwell's—dear Jamey. What an awful thing to happen—Faith Oldham had seemed polite. Shy, not at all certain of herself, saying little—but polite. So she would say, "Of course, Mrs. North. I realize that," not, in fact, realizing it at all, or believing it at all.

"It's really true," Pam would say then. "Oh, murder cases happen to us. I can't deny that. But it isn't the other way around. Whatever Inspector O'Malley thinks."

Only, Pam thought—getting up from the dressing table and going to the living room, with Martini trotting behind her, waiting for a lap to settle—only I won't bring the inspector into it. The trouble with me is, I'm so likely to say the one phrase too many. So as to make things clear. And people do seem to get confused so easily.

She was just going into the living room when the buzzer sounded. Martha popped out of the kitchen door at the other end of the room, saw Mrs. North and popped back in again. Pam opened the room, looked up at Faith Oldham and said, "Good morning."

"It's so good of you—" the tall girl said—the tall, too-thin girl with startled blue eyes in a fragile face; the somehow gawky girl; the girl who seemed to live in an unfamiliar world. Pam North, who is no handshaker by habit, nevertheless reached out a slim hand to the girl's larger, thinner, very long-fingered hand.

"It isn't at all," Pam said, and drew Faith Oldham into the room, and said, "Sit there—" and then, just in time, *"No.* Wait a minute," and lifted Martini out of the "there" chair. Martini sat on the floor and, indignantly, licked her left shoulder.

"If it's her chair," Faith Oldham said.

"All the chairs we've got are her chairs," Pam said. "If we went by that, we'd stand all the time."

"She's very pretty," Faith said.

Pam looked at Martini.

"Yes," she said. "Even with the hole in her head."

It is not actually a hole, although so referred to. It is more in the nature of a wart. Martini does not mind having it mentioned.

Faith Oldham looked puzzled.

"Never mind," Pam said. "You know, Miss Oldham, Jerry and I aren't detectives." And the rest of it, as envisioned, including the inspector, although resolved against.

"Mrs. North," Faith said, "I've—I've got to talk to somebody. And there isn't anybody—and—I keep feeling it's my fault and—" She seemed, suddenly, on the verge of crying. She knotted her thin hands together in her lap.

"I don't—" Pam said.

"If I'd been there when I was supposed to be," Faith Oldham said. "Not let mother—just gone anyway—don't you see?" Her eyes were very wide, questioning.

Pam's mind hurried. This tall—this touching—girl appealed for help, but appealed thinking Pam knew more than she knew, could respond more quickly. And now a question would seem—cold, unresponding. It would seem as if she did not want to help when—

Pam's mind hurried over what Bill had told them. Of course—

"Of course," she said. "Had met Mr. Hunter at the bookshop at three. But my dear—"

"Mrs. North," Faith said, "I know what all of you think—Captain Weigand and you and Mr. North and everybody. And—it *isn't true*. Carl couldn't do a thing like that. And—why would he? Jamey was his friend. Jamey was helping him. You don't know how much. And to think that he'd—he'd—"

This time she did cry. She groped in her purse blindly and pulled out a draggled bit of tissue and dabbed at her eyes with the tissue.

"We're so alone," the girl said, her soft, low voice watery too, uneven. "Now with Jamey gone and—" She did not finish.

"Listen, dear," Pam said. "Bill—that's Captain Weigand—doesn't think Mr. Hunter killed Jamey. At least, I'm sure he doesn't."

"I know he *does*," Faith said. "And Hope's right— why shouldn't they think that, when he was there—or could have been there—?"

Hope? Oh, of course. Faith called her mother by her given name. When childen did that—

"Wait a minute," Pam said. "Tea or coffee?"

The girl looked at her.

"Elevenses," Pam said. "I always do."

Which is not true; which then seemed a good idea.

Faith didn't care which. She did not seem to think about it. She looked at her twisted hands.

"Just sit still," Pam said. "Here—have a cigarette."

The girl shook her head.

Pam walked the length of the room, poked her head into the kitchen, said, "Coffee please, Martha," and came back. The girl had not moved. Pam lighted a cigarette and said it wouldn't be a moment.

"I shouldn't have come," Faith said, rather suddenly. "I—I just had to talk to somebody. Somebody whose mind wasn't already—made up. Because if I had been at the bookshop at three we could *prove*—"

"Of course you should have come," Pam said. "And nobody really thinks Mr. Hunter had anything to do with it."

She spoke firmly. And, she thought, I'd better cross my fingers, since I don't know what Bill thinks. Except that, if he didn't, Bill won't think he did.

"They do," Faith said. "All of you do. And Hope— She keeps saying she told me he wasn't—"

"Whatever your mother's told you," Pam said. "She doesn't know any more about it than anybody else." The girl looked at her with eyes very large. "Of course she doesn't," Pam said, in the tone—she trusted—of an oracle. "Now—"

Martha came in with a tray, with two cups steaming. Instant, obviously, in so little time. Well, instant was all right.

"Drink your coffee," Pam told Faith Oldham, and demonstrated by sipping hers. Yes, instant. Good enough, though.

"Now," Pam said. "So far as I know, all there is against Mr. Hunter is that he was with Jamey a little while before somebody shot Jamey. And—I suppose there's nobody else at the bookshop who remembers seeing him?"

That supposition was reasonably obvious. It seemed, nevertheless, momentarily to startle Faith. Then she said that that was just it. There had been a lot of people at the bookshop, but none Hunter knew, and he had not bought anything, or even spoken to any of the clerks. It was just a place to meet—one waited to meet, and browsed and—

"We all do it," Faith said. "And—get interested in what we're reading and don't notice other people and—"

"Mr. Hunter's tried to find somebody who remembers seeing him there? At the right time?"

"Yes. And—there isn't anybody."

"Look," Pam said. "Mr. Hunter—he was one of Jamey's—subjects? You know what I mean?"

"Jamey hypnotized him," the girl said. "Yes. He did—lots of people. Mrs. North—there isn't anything wrong in that. It doesn't—do anything to people. Weaken their wills or—or anything. All that's—superstition." She was anxious. "Really like—" She looked around. Martini was sitting and looking up at her, distantly. "Like the belief that cats suck the breath of babies," she said.

"That's nonsense," Pam said, warmly. "And that they're any more sly than anybody else. And that they don't love people and—some woman said once they don't even *recognize* people. Somebody who was supposed to *know*. A *psychologist*. And I don't believe she had ever *met* a cat. Why, Martini—"

Pam North managed to stop herself.

"About hypnotism," she said, bringing herself back. "I've read a little in Jamey's book. That is, anyway, Jerry has and's told me. It's nothing against Mr. Hunter that he let Jamey hypnotize him. Doesn't mean a thing about him."

"Except," Faith said—and now she was drinking her coffee, now she reached out and took a cigarette from a box—"except that he's one of those who can be. About one in five can. Nobody seems to know why. Why the percentage, I mean. Or, actually, how it works—one man thinks it's some kind of conditioned reflex."

It occurred to Pam that they were in danger of riding their respective hobbyhorses in different directions. This might, momentarily, take Faith Oldham's mind off Hunter; it appeared that, momentarily, it had. But it did not, on the other hand, get them any place.

"Faith," Pam said. "You wouldn't be so worried—I don't think you would—about Mr. Hunter if you didn't think he—well, that he might have had some reason to kill Jamey."

The girl leaned forward. She seemed about to stand up. The blue eyes changed, seemed somehow to intensify.

"If you think that—" she said, and her voice changed too. It was deeper, more vibrant.

"Wait a minute," Pam said. "Wait a minute. You came here to—talk about this. Because, you said, you were—what did you say?—so alone. So, I suppose, because you wanted help. Isn't that right?"

"I don't know," the girl said. "You and Mr. North seemed—like people who would understand. And once Jamey said something about your having had experience in things like this. And then I thought I could find out—"

"I know," Pam said. "How things were going. As concerning Mr. Hunter. Well—I've told you what I know about that. And I'm ready to help—anyway, to talk about it. But we can't if you won't."

"I'm sorry," Faith said. "No, I don't know any

reason Carl could have had—any motive. And, I know he wouldn't do a thing like that anyway. And—I know that that isn't good enough. Is it?"

"No," Pam said. "Faith—did you know that Jamey—wasn't well? That, actually, he didn't have much longer to live?"

The girl looked at her. The full blue eyes seemed, to Pam, to narrow a little. She said, "Why?"

"You did, didn't you?" Pam said, taking a chance.

Faith hesitated.

"I didn't—know," she said. "I was, from things he said—not definite things but—as if he were resigned—yes, I was afraid of it. But—why?"

"Oh," Pam said. "I—wondered if you knew. In a way, it makes what's happened—well, easier to accept, doesn't it? You were fond—very fond—of Jamey. I know that. Even Jerry and I, although we only knew him a few months—"

It wasn't, Pam thought, particularly good. But it was as far as she wanted to go. Unless the girl herself—

"That really isn't why you brought it up, is it?" Faith said. She was much steadier now; that, at any rate, had been gained. "What you meant was—Jamey didn't have any real reason to live. It was going to be—painful?"

"I think so," Pam said.

"That he could—have arranged for somebody to make it—quicker? Easier? By—using hypnotism?"

"I don't think it's possible," Pam said. "I think that all of the authorities think it isn't—*Faith!*"

The girl had dropped her face in her hands. Her body shook. She said, "I'm afraid. I'm *afraid.*"

And, Pam North was startled; obscurely upset. The night's theory had become, with morning, only a theory of the night, grotesquely contorted, as are the thoughts of night. At breakfast, only a few hours before, she and Jerry had agreed on that, and been somewhat amused at themselves. And Jerry had, again, explained to both of them that all the authorities Jameson Elwell, who was himself one, cited agreed that there was no proof a person in hypnosis would not reject, out of hand, instruction to perpetrate any serious crime. And here the girl—

"There's no reason to be afraid," Pam said. "Not of that, anyway. At least I—"

Now the girl changed again; she was a changeable girl.

"They don't really know," she said. "Oh, for years all the authorities were pretty much agreed that a person couldn't be made to commit any crime. Let alone to kill. But lately—well, they're not so sure. I've been helping—had been helping Jamey with research. Getting quotations and things like that. From—" She named names Pam North had never heard—Wells, Rowland, Estabrooks. A good many now thought merely that certain things were unproved, not that they were impossible.

"Take this man Salter,"* Faith Oldham said, and Pam shook her head slowly, being unable to take something she had never heard of. "He's very certain a good subject could be made to do—anything. And

---

* Andrew Salter (*What Is Hypnosis?* Farrar, Straus and Cudahy, Inc., 1955): "Put bluntly, through hypnosis it is possible to force persons to commit crimes. Those who speak of the necessity for hypnotic suggestion to fit in with a subject's 'moral code' should revise their concepts. . . . My comments advocating the possibility of the hypnotic production of crimes have aroused the opposition of pollyannas who know nothing about the matter."

Professor Estabrooks,† although he doesn't go as far, says that while he doesn't claim that *all* good subjects would commit crimes, it seems 'highly probable' that many would."

"Oh," Pam North said. Faith was looking at her with very wide—clearly, Pam thought, very frightened—eyes. And Pam, if not precisely frightened, was definitely uneasy. It proved, she thought briefly, the folly of shooting arrows into the air, not knowing where they might come down. "Well," Pam North said. The girl waited.

"Even if he could he wouldn't," Pam said. "Jamey, I mean." And waited, with growing uneasiness, for an echo—for corroboration from a person who clearly knew a good deal about this mysterious matter—of her own grotesque theory of the night.

And—it did not come.

"Of course he wouldn't have," Faith said. "Anybody who knew him would know that. Only—they wouldn't have known him. All those people—your friend Captain Weigand and—I don't know—lawyers and people on a jury and—he would just be a name and Carl would—would be another and nobody would *really* know."

"I—" Pam said.

"I know," Faith said. "You think I'm frightened because—because I think Carl was hypnotized and

_____

† G. H. Estabrooks (*Hypnotism*. E. P. Dutton & Company, 1943). The passage to which Faith apparently refers is: "The reader must bear in mind that we do not claim *all* good hypnotic subjects would commit a criminal act as the result of hypnotism. Far from it. We only assert that, from the evidence we have, it seems highly probable that many subjects would do so if urged on by a good operator." (P. 167.)

made to kill Jamey. I *don't*. I don't and I never will, because Jamey wouldn't do a thing like that to anybody and Carl wouldn't—I don't care what they say— if everybody in the world said—"

Then, again, she buried her face in her hands. Pam started to get up from the chair, to go to her, and Faith's hands went down and she shook her head.

"I'm sorry," she said. "I'm all right. It's—not that I'm afraid about what *has* happened. That's all right— about Carl it's all right. I'm afraid of what *can* happen. Because—they'll think of this, won't they? Even people who don't know anything about hypnotism—think it's something that used to go on on the stage, and a man with glittering eyes swinging a watch back and forth—" There was contempt in the young voice; the contempt of young knowledge for ancient myth. "—even they'll think of this. Because now even doctors are beginning to understand it, and magazines to print articles about it."

"I imagine," Pam said, "that they'll—well, try everything else first. Because, you take a jury—"

She paused, considering.

"Jurys like things simple," Pam said. "Nobody gives them a thing that's hard to believe if there's any other way."

(Bill must have told me that, sometime, Pam North thought.)

"But this isn't hard to—" Faith said, and did not finish.

"Not for you," Pam said. "You obviously know lots about it. Helping in Jamey's experiments and everything—working with him. I wonder—how does it feel to be hypnotized?"

"How?" Faith said. "Oh—Jamey never hypnotized

me, Mrs. North. Not because I wasn't willing. I just wasn't one of those who can be hypnotized. Maybe I'm not bright enough." She almost smiled; a watery almost-smile. "There's probably some correlation between intelligence and susceptibility," she said. "Anyway, the feeble-minded can't be hypnotized, or almost never can. Oh—he could get me to relax and feel sleepy. And then he'd say, 'Your eyelids are locked tightly together. You cannot open them.' And—I'd open them. Every time. So—"

She stopped talking and stood up. She looked at her watch and said she must go now.

She said, "Mrs. North. It was good of you to let me talk. I—I guess I just needed to talk to somebody. And— I know there's no way you can help us but—"

Pam stood too.

"Only," Faith Oldham said. "I don't know how to ask this. Probably I shouldn't. But—almost the worst thing is not knowing. What they—what they're thinking, planning to do. I don't ask you to—I know Captain Weigand's a friend. I know you can't—"

She found it hard to say, obviously. And there was no clear answer, obviously.

"Bill's fair," Pam said. "Without me—without anybody. And—he doesn't jump at things, Faith. All the same, I'll be as much a—a friend at court as I can."

It wasn't much. But the girl nodded her head slowly, acceptingly. And the large blue eyes did not, now, seem quite so strained, so frightened.

7

Pam was late; she was looked at from under raised eyebrows, by Jerry and Bill Weigand. Their expressions chided. The expression on the wide face of Sergeant Mullins was, Pam thought briefly, more one of apprehension.

They had acquired a sofa and a chair—which Mullins slightly overflowed—in a corner of the Algonquin lobby. As she approached, Pam saw Jerry's hand go out to a little bell on a table, and heard the bell tinkle. So that was being taken care of. A waiter looked at the bell, at Mrs. North, and said, "With House of Lords," and went away. Which was pleasant if, perhaps, and viewed in a certain light, an incident to give pause.

"Martini got in the elevator," Pam said, and sat down on the sofa between Bill Weigand and Jerry. "Did you tell him, Jerry?"

"Wait," Jerry said. "If you mean Raul, he says five minutes. So we'll have time for a couple. If you mean Bill, partly. And what do you mean, 'in the elevator'?"

"Jerry," Pam said. "You know the elevator! Martini got in it, somehow. I never know how, when you're looking right at her, she disappears and turns up places. And the new boy is afraid of cats and did something wrong and we stuck. And Teeney yowled, because it turns out she doesn't like elevators. I suppose she thinks the bottom's falling out."

Mullins closed his eyes. He took a firm grip on an old-fashioned glass and raised the glass steadily to his lips.

"Probably," Jerry said. "Sometimes I feel the same—*stuck?*"

"Oh," Pam said, "not seriously. He's an ailurophobe and you know how Teeney feels about them. Incidentally, I do think they ought to have asked us first, don't you? Because with one of those on the elevator—"

"Stuck?" Jerry said. "Stuck?"

"Only a few minutes," Pam said. "Then I ran it back up myself—he just stood in a corner and said, 'No. *No!*'—and put Teeney in, but by then I had a run and—none of this is important, really. Faith Oldham can't be hypnotized. So I guess it's false pretenses, Bill. But very nice all the same. Thank you." The last was to the waiter, for a martini with the glass dewed with chill. "Now—where are we?"

"That, Pam, is quite a question," Bill Weigand said. "Jerry told me about the theory you two ran up. But—you say she can't be hypnotized?"

"She says not," Pam said. "And—I don't think she's lying. But on the other hand, she herself rather changed our horses. She's afraid—"

Pam told them what Faith Oldham was afraid of. It

was, she pointed out, very much the same thing. "Only, the other side out."

Sergeant Mullins took a still firmer grip on his old-fashioned glass. He spoke slowly, heavily.

"Listen, Mrs. North," he said. "There ain't—there isn't any such thing as hypnotism. It's all a con game." He looked at Weigand, at Jerry North, and there was a kind of entreaty in his eyes. "Everybody knows that," he said. "It's a trick. Like sawing a woman in two."* His expression now was one of deep anxiety. "You know that, Loot," he said, and it was indicative of his perturbation that he did not correct himself.

Bill looked at Jerry North. Both shook their heads. "I'm sorry, sergeant," Bill Weigand said.

"Listen, Loot," Mullins said. He did not go on. He put his old-fashioned glass down on the table. Like a man in a dream, then, he reached out and tapped the little, tinkling bell.

Bill Weigand looked at Jerry, who shrugged.

"That's all," he said. "I've told you Pam's theory.

---

* Mullins's disbelief is perhaps still shared by many; it was once almost universal, and in unexpected places. Dr. Ian Stevenson, professor and chairman of the Department of Psychiatry, University of Virginia School of Medicine, writes (*Harper's,* November, 1958) that Dr. James Esdaile, a surgeon of the 1840's who had performed many successful operations on patients in hypnosis, "had great difficulty in getting his work even published, much less accepted. His scientific critics alleged that he had bribed his patients to sham insensibility. According to one account 'it was because they were hardened impostors that they let their legs be cut off and large tumors be cut out without showing any sign even of discomfort.' In their opposition to hypnotism many of the most creative scientists of the period forgot the rules of their own calling. Lord Kelvin announced that 'one-half of hypnotism is imposture and the rest bad observation.' "

And my alternative. This—this other side of it doesn't change anything, really."

"Except people," Pam said. "They might think that that—"

"It is hard to believe," Bill said. "I'll give Mullins that."

Mullins remained in reverie. A waiter came; Mullins merely pointed at his almost empty glass.

"All Elwell says," Jerry said, "is that a good many tests suggest that a good subject can be prevailed upon to do almost anything. And none of them is conclusive in proving murder isn't included. And—there's one other thing. There are a good many tricks a good operator can play on his subjects. One of them is to wipe out all memory of ever having been hypnotized. Another is to plant in their minds the belief they can't be. So, Miss Oldham can be telling what she thinks to be the truth about herself but—"

"Jerry," Pam said. "You never told me that."

Jameson Elwell's book was, Jerry said, a rather long book. He did not contend that he had told her everything in it If she wanted to read it—"And," he said, "I brought you a copy, Bill."

He put a thick book on the little table. Mullins moved his glass slightly away from the book.

"You can't," Pam said, "argue we're not co-operating. Co-operate back."

The waiter brought Mullins's old-fashioned. He was sent away for more martinis. Raul came from the restaurant entrance and looked around the lobby. He looked at the group in the corner. The group seemed as contented as any maitre d' could wish. He went in search of another quartet.

"Right," Bill said. "Let's skip this business of hypnotism for a moment. Let the sergeant get back on his feet. So—"

They could, as it happened, skip it without necessarily skipping either Carl Hunter or Faith Oldham. Faith stood to inherit a quarter of Jameson Elwell's estate. Jameson Elwell's estate might run as high as half a million dollars. Judging by their attitudes when together, and by Faith's visit to Pam, they might well be planning marriage. Q.E.D.

"Did they know about it?" Pam asked.

Bill could not be positive, not yet.

Hunter had been unable to find anyone who had seen him in the bookshop, waiting for Faith, at three o'clock the previous afternoon for the simplest of reasons—he wasn't in it. Mullins—Mullins stirred faintly at the mention of his name—had found a clerk who knew Hunter well and was certain that he had come into the shop not earlier than three-fifteen. Which would have given him time enough, if he had been lucky with taxicabs. Confronted with this, Hunter had said that, O.K., he was not precisely in the shop, but was standing in front of it. Asked why, he had said, "Because it was a nice day."

"Well," Pam said, "it was a nice day. Which side of the street is the shop on?"

"Oh," Bill said, "he'd have been standing in the sun, all right. If he was standing in front of the shop. And Miss Oldham got there about the time he says she did—about five minutes after he did go into the shop."

"Timetables," Pam North said, in discontentment.

Bill said he was sorry, but there they were.

The professor's brother, Foster Elwell, did not stand to inherit anything, but three of his children did. He told them about Foster Elwell, briefly. He had lunched, at the Pierre Grill, with the man he said he had lunched with. But the man thought he had left there about two-thirty. Again—lucky with taxicabs.

There was also a man named Rosco Finch. He told them, as briefly as possible, about Finch—about Finch and the activities of Investigators, Inc., at the behest of Professor Elwell. And of Finch's lonely practicing of drives at a country club in Connecticut.

It appeared, on the basis of enquiries made, on request, by the Connecticut State Police that Mr. Finch's practice must have been very lonely indeed. At least, the few members of the club staff on duty did not remember seeing him. So lonely, it appeared, one might almost read invisible. However—

"There," Pam North said, "will always be a however, won't there?"

There would—however, the clubhouse was some distance from the first tee, and there was no special reason to think Finch would have driven from the first tee. The club had a largely commuter membership; the time was midweek, the time was also midautumn when golf courses in Connecticut are likely to lie unused under the brightest sun. So, Rosco Finch might well have done what he said he had done and done it unobserved.

"The more important thing," Pam said. "Yes, Raul?"

"Your table is ready," Raul said. "If you are ready."

Pam stood up. She held her cocktail glass. Raul shook his head, gently. Pam put her glass down. Raul carried several menus in his right hand. He slapped them against his left palm. A waiter, obviously not there an instant before, materialized, rather as if out of a bottle. The waiter put the four drinks on a tray and stood at attention.

"Come in," Raul said, and they went in, went to a table from which Raul flicked a sign which said "Reserved." The drinks were apportioned, according to need and previous possessor.

"—is," Pam North said, "was he actually driving the car? You talked to him, sergeant?"

The short walk seemed to have revived Sergeant Mullins.

"There isn't any evidence," Sergeant Mullins said. "He says no he wasn't, like he has from the start. You can't give a guess to a jury, on account of it's not legal." He paused to sip from his glass. "Ten to one," Mullins said, "he was driving and had had a couple and went to sleep." He considered. "Twenty to one," he said. "And no way I can see to prove it."

"The other question," Jerry said, "did he know this Investigators whatever-it-is was working for Professor Elwell?"

"Probably," Sergeant Mullins said, and finished his drink. "He could have guessed."

Pam counted by tapping the fingers of her right hand on the tablecloth. She said it seemed to come to four, already. "Faith," she said, "Mr. Hunter, Jamey's brother, now this Mr. Finch." She shook her head. "Four makes a clutter," Pam said. "And to think that such a dear as poor Jamey—" She did not finish the obvious, as she often does not. She sighed and shook her head again.

Which, Bill Weigand said, brought up a point. Were they sure that Professor Jameson Elwell had been all they thought he was? The kindly, generous man they thought he was?

113

"Bill!" Pam said, in protest. "Of course he was."

Bill looked at Jerry North.

"I certainly thought so," Jerry said. "In our dealings with him at the office, in what Pam and I saw of him outside—yes. Of course—" He shrugged, the shrug saying that certainty in such matters was not so easily to be achieved. *"Jerry!"* Pam North said, speaking to a Judas. Jerry smiled at her and she took an indignant sip from her martini glass. "I take it," Jerry said to Bill, "that you've come across a minority report?"

Bill had. He summarized briefly. Pam said that it was outrageous, that she didn't believe a word of it and that there must be something the matter with Mrs. Oldham to make her say things like that. She also hoped that Bill didn't believe such nonsense for a moment.

"You have ordered?" Raul said. They had not; they did. "Something light," Pam said. "Oh—it's corned beef and cabbage day. Corned beef and cabbage, Raul." She turned to Mullins. "It's always wonderful," she told Mullins. "A chef's salad, I guess," Mullins said.

Bill did not believe or disbelieve. A new field had, certainly, been opened by Mrs. Oldham's assertions. Suppose the assertions merely spiteful; suppose them untrue. The matter had still to be looked into, since the character of a victim is always a central factor of a crime. So—so he had gone to talk to Eugene Wahmsley, dean of faculty, at Dyckman.

He had found a central room on the sixth floor of the administration building—a room with a rail across it, and an efficient middle-aged woman at a desk beyond the rail, and several typewriters clicking; an office in all respects very businesslike. And Professor Wahmsley would, certainly, see Captain Weigand, who was expected. If Captain Weigand would come this way?

He went, through a gate, across the big room, to a corner office. Wahmsley stood up behind a desk and asked Weigand how things were coming, and what he could do to make them come better, if that was, as he assumed it was, the idea.

"Dr. Wahmsley," Bill said, "is it possible that Professor Elwell was not—not all he appeared to be? All people seemed to think he was?"

He was told that that was an unexpected question; he was invited to sit down; he was offered and accepted a cigarette.

"Anything is possible, I suppose," Wahmsley said, then. "If you want my opinion—I've already given you my opinion. Elwell was a brilliant man. He was a good man. I take it you've come across another opinion?"

"Yes," Bill said. "Is it possible that Professor Elwell appropriated the ideas of other people?"

"Oh," Wahmsley said. "He built on what was already there. There's no other way I've ever heard of. But—appropriated? I suppose you mean without credit? Without—" And then, abruptly, he stopped. "Oh," he said. "Hope Oldham."

"Right," Bill said. "Mrs. Oldham."

Wahmsley said he might have known. He inhaled thoughtfully, he exhaled with decision. He said that he could, he supposed, guess what Mrs. Oldham had said. That the ideas in Elwell's books were really the stolen ideas of Professor Frank Oldham? That Elwell's apparent kindness to Hope Oldham and her daughter was the grudging product of a guilty conscience? That Jameson Elwell had been, in effect, a fraud?

"Yes," Bill said. "Also that Elwell played the stock market on Oldham's advice, which seems to make Mrs. Oldham feel that the money is really hers. Also, in some fashion not very clear to me, that Elwell took advantage of the innocence of the girl—Faith."

"Hope Oldham," Wahmsley said, "is a strange case. Perhaps not really a strange case. I've known others like her. Probably you have, too. Any lack of success is due, not to any personal lack of ability to achieve success, but to—to the chicanery of others. You know the type?"

Bill nodded his head.

"As to the specific charges," Wahmsley said. "The first—that Elwell absconded with Oldham's abstract ideas. That's nonsense. They weren't even in the same field, you know. Oh—cognate fields, in a sense. Philosophy and psychology. But all fields in which the mind is concerned are to some extent cognate, aren't they?"

"I'd suppose so," Bill said.

"Before poor Frank died," Wahmsley said, "his wife used now and then to—hint things like that. It embarrassed Frank a good deal. Among other things, it was, in a back-handed sort of fashion, an apology for Frank. And Frank needed apologizing for about as little as any man I've ever known. I told you that—we considered him one of our—well, say, stars. Oldham of Dyckman. So it was so pointless, so much without meaning."

"Then why—" Bill began, but Wahmsley did not encourage him to finish.

Wahmsley said, "Precisely, captain. There are, as we all know, different criteria of success. Oldham certainly did not make as much money as his wife would have liked. Not, I'm afraid, by a very long way. A professor's salary—well, you've heard about professors' salaries, no doubt. The royalties from publications in the field of philosophy are not exorbitant. As you probably would guess. And I'm afraid that, in all financial matters, Oldham was a babe in arms. Which answers your question about Elwell acting on his friend's advice. To put it bluntly, Jamey would have had more sense—did have more sense."

"Did Oldham share his wife's opinions? You suggest he didn't but—"

"I'm quite sure he didn't," Wahmsley said. "Oh, I've no doubt she suggested he did. I certainly never saw anything to indicate he did. I find it difficult to imagine that anything like that would ever have occurred to Oldham. As far as she is concerned—"

This time he interrupted himself. He got up and walked to a window and looked through the window. He came back. He said he might as well tell Weigand something else.

When Oldham died, and it was found out that he had left his wife and young daughter inadequately provided for, Dyckman had felt responsibility. "We," Wahmsley said, and did not specify further. There were at Dyckman, as at any other large university, a number of administrative jobs to be filled—from file clerks to student interviewers. "It's amazing how much of a kind of superior clerical work there is to be done in a place like this," Wahmsley said.

Briefly, a job had been found for Mrs. Oldham—a

job in which no special skills were needed, except the special skill of being intelligent. She did not have to file, to type; she did not have to make decisions of major importance. But she had to make some decisions, to meet a good many people and listen to them, and understand them.

"Well," Wahmsley said, "we made all the allowances we could, because of the special circumstances. More than we would have made for most. You don't want details but—say we finally had to admit to ourselves that Hope Oldham just wouldn't do. That there wasn't any place we could fit her in. And—not because she isn't intelligent. She is, in her way. But it's not, I'm afraid, a very—useful way. And she proved to be very difficult to get along with. A certain—call it give and take—is necessary in a place like this, as I suppose it is everywhere. Hope Oldham, I'm afraid—" He did not finish that sentence. He said, "We had to let her go."

"And?"

"It was quite unpleasant," Wahmsley said. "At least—I wasn't too directly involved, but I gather it was. A good many—charges. As one would expect, of course. Where things had gone wrong, it was because of failures of other people. Or, in one or two instances, the fact that they cheated. All very unpleasant. And, I'm not quite sure why I've told you all this. Except— well, they say every little bit helps."

As to Elwell's having, in any fashion, taken advantage of Faith Oldham's inexperience—Wahmsley found that flatly unbelievable. As a matter of fact, from what he knew of the girl—which wasn't much—he thought her a much more competent young woman than one might judge from her rather fragile appearance.

"Childlike outwardly," Wahmsley said. "I should doubt she is inwardly. But, I've only met her a few times. She's scholastically quite superior, if that means anything." He looked at Weigand through blue smoke. "Which I'm not at all certain it does," he said.

Bill Weigand told part of this to the Norths, at their table at the Algonquin. Pam nodded her head, holding a forkful of corned beef in abeyance.

"I know the type," she said. "The poor things. If at first you don't succeed, blame, blame again. Of course, they do stir up trouble. Which I suppose satisfies something." She conveyed corned beef to mouth.

Pam swallowed. She said, with that completed, that she had once known a girl who was very much like Mrs. Oldham.

"She was always losing out on things," Pam said. "Jobs, mostly. And always because people were against her or crooked in some way. She knew an awful lot of crooked people, the poor thing. Hearing her talk about people was like—" Pam paused. "Like being in one of those places with the funny mirrors. Everything was always out of drawing. Except, of course, she wasn't herself. After you'd heard her talk awhile you got dizzy."

She looked around the table at the three men, who looked at her with speculation.

"Only," Mullins said, "there has to be something to get reflected, Mrs. North. In these mirrors of yours."

They waited.

"All right," Pam said, "we'll break the mirrors, sergeant."

But both Jerry and Bill shook their heads. After a moment, Pam shook hers, also.

"And," Bill pointed out, "the fact that a person always blames somebody else for his failure doesn't prove that there is never anybody else to blame."

"I realize that," Pam said. "Sometimes there is a wolf. Granted. But Jamey wasn't."

"Actually," Jerry said, "you don't believe what she said about Elwell either, Bill. Or, is it time for the one about smoke and fire?"

"Of course," Pam said, "somebody could read all Professor Elwell's books and all Professor Oldham's and that way—"

She stopped, observing that her words froze as they fell.

"She said another thing," Bill told them. "Mrs. Oldham, I mean. That there wasn't anything between her daughter and Carl Hunter. Except that the girl was 'sorry' for young Hunter. Why she should be, not disclosed. That there was another young man. Name disclosed. Arnold Ames. One of 'the' Ameses."

"Is he?" That was Pam.

There was an Arnold Ames listed in the *Social Register*. He was the son of Mr. and Mrs. Wellington Ames. Wellington Ames was important in a bank. Wellington Ames's father had been important in a bank.

"I can have a theory," Pam said.

"I'm sure," Jerry said.

"Jamey was influencing Faith against Mr. Ames. Mr. Ames found out and killed him. Mr. Ames is very much in love with Faith, of course."

"He'd rather need to be," Jerry said, but looked at Bill. Bill grinned slightly, and shook his head.

"Having seen the girl and Hunter together," Bill said, "I doubt Mrs. Oldham is—let's say well informed. I suppose somebody'll have to have a little chat with this Ames scion to keep things tidy. But—"

Raul approached, the handkerchief in his breast pocket a banner. He said that Captain Weigand was wanted on the telephone.

"I never," Bill said, "seem to get to stay for coffee." He went. He was gone several minutes and, as he walked between tables, he jerked his head upward at Mullins, and Mullins finished his coffee in a gulp and stood up.

"Young Hunter's been shot," Bill said. "Wounded. They don't know how seriously. Taken to Dyckman Hospital."

Pam North looked shocked.

"I only meant it to be a theory," she said.

Jerry's question was more immediate.

"Where?" he said. "And I don't mean anatomically."

"Half a block from the Elwell house," Bill said. "He seems to have been going in that direction." Then he said, "Come on, Mullins," and they went on.

8

Carl Hunter had been shot, from behind, in the right leg, as he was walking toward the two Elwell houses at around eleven-thirty in the morning. He had been shot just after he had passed the mouth of a service passageway four doors up the sloping street from his destination, his destination being the house the Oldhams lived in; his purpose being to pick Faith up and take her to lunch—an early lunch, since she had a one o'clock class. He had no idea whatever who had shot him, or why anybody would want to.

He had been out of surgery for more than an hour when Bill Weigand and Mullins reached the hospital; he was in a private room.

"Lost a bit of blood," the resident said. "Feel groggy for a while. Nothing serious. Missed the bone. Sure you can talk to him. He may be a little vague."

He did not seem to be especially vague; more than anything else, he seemed annoyed. Which was understandable. "Right at a crucial point with the cats," he said, "and this has to happen. Probably have to start the whole damn series over again."

Surely he had some idea who might have wanted to shoot him, presumably to kill him? It could hardly be to interrupt his "series" with the cats.

"Mr. Hunter," Bill said, "do you know more than you've told us about the professor's death?"

"Oh," Carl Hunter said, "I've been thinking about that. Jumps to the mind, doesn't it?"

"Right," Bill said. "Well?"

"Nothing," Hunter said. His gray eyes were entirely steady. "I told you what I know—which is nothing. I was there; I went away anyway fifteen minutes before you say he was killed. All right—I stood outside the bookshop instead of going in right away. And—that doesn't mean anything."

"Who," Bill said, "do you know that's a good shot, Mr. Hunter? Or, assuming killing you was what was planned, a not very good shot?"

"Nobody," Hunter said. "Fact is, I don't know anybody's got a gun of any kind, or knows how to use one. Or would use one."

He smiled, faintly.

"I know a very peaceable lot," he said. "Wouldn't hurt a fly."

"Or a cat?"

"My God no," he said. "The cats have a fine time."

"You were walking down the street and there was a bang—I suppose you did hear the gun go off?"

"Yes," Hunter said. "It didn't make a lot of noise and I was—it was as if somebody had kicked me in the leg, as much as anything else. I fell down and this man of yours—the patrolman outside the professor's house—came running. Did a spot of first aid; got an ambulance on the double. Very efficient man, luckily for me. Might have lain there and drained dry, for all I know."

"You didn't see anybody. In the block?"

"Sure. Down at the far end, near the drive, there was a woman pushing a baby carriage. On the other side of the street, there was somebody parking a car. It isn't a busy block, captain. I realize I'm not helping much." His eyes were very intelligent. "Tell me they got the bullet," he said. "Doesn't it answer any questions?"

They didn't know yet. The calibre was right.

"Obviously," Hunter said, "you haven't caught anybody."

They had not. They had found the service passageway; found that it led to the unfenced back yards of several houses; found, also, that from them passageways ran to the parallel street beyond. Hunter nodded. "I know," he said. "It's rather like a park—community effort. And nobody waiting to give himself up?"

Nobody had been.

"Mr. Hunter," Bill said, "did Professor Elwell ever hypnotize Miss Oldham?"

"What the hell?" Hunter said. "What's that got to do with—anything?"

"Did he?"

"So far as I know, no," Hunter said. "As a matter of fact, she believes she's not a subject. And I don't know why Jamey would—" He stopped, a little abruptly.

"Establish amnesia?"

"You've been reading books, captain," Hunter said, and seemed slightly amused. "Yes, that's what I meant."

"He didn't with you?"

"No. I see you've been finding things out."

Bill nodded his head.

"I'm rather a good subject," Carl Hunter said. "I suppose you think that means—" He let it go, as of no importance. "No, amnesia didn't enter into it. In a sense it was a—a collaboration."

"Why did you break the clock?"

"Oh—that. Posthypnotic suggestion. Followed by rationalization. To avoid looking like a fool."

"Mr. Hunter, could a man like yourself—a good subject—be directed, under hypnosis, to do—anything?"

"*Anything?*"

Bill nodded his head.

"I doubt it," Hunter said. "So did Jamey. I don't argue anybody knows. So that—well, it's nothing to meddle with. Nothing for amateurs to meddle with. And, what are you getting at?"

"Anything I can," Bill said. "About Professor Elwell and—the people around him. For example—can you tell me anything about a man named Ames? Arnold Ames?"

Hunter was propped in the hospital bed. He moved slightly and said, "Ouch," with no particular emphasis. He said, "Captain, I'll tell you anything I can to help clear this up. Anything that has any bearing. But if you're just fishing around—and if Faith is going to be dragged into it—"

"Obviously I'm fishing," Weigand said. "And nobody'll be dragged into it who isn't in it."

Hunter looked at Bill Weigand for some seconds.

"All right," he said. "Ames is a man who used to date Faith. Up to three-four months ago. I met him a couple of times. Upstanding citizen, and a lot of money in the family." He smiled faintly. "The kind who could be the apple of Hope Oldman's eye."

"And was?"

"Oh yes," Hunter said. "And I'm not. And—nothing could be of less importance, captain. Whatever you're getting at."

You do not push too long in the same place.

"Right," Bill said. "How about a man named Finch? Rosco Finch?"

"Poor Liz's boyfriend," Hunter said. "Yes—I ran into him a few times, too. At the Elwell house. Golf pro. Of all the silly ways to live. And I'm damned if I see—" He stopped and his intelligent gray eyes narrowed somewhat. "The accident come into it?"

"I don't know that it does. Or, that it doesn't."

Hunter again looked at Bill Weigand for some seconds.

"Jamey thought Finch was driving," Hunter said. "I gather you've come on that, somehow."

"He told you that?"

"Yes. I was nearer their age—Liz's anyway. Finch has got several years on me. How did I think their minds worked? Particularly Finch's mind."

"And?"

"I said I hadn't the foggiest notion how a golfer's mind works. Probably said I doubted if they worked as well as cats'. And that I knew a lot more about cats."

"Seriously?"

"No. But I knew Finch very slightly. I've nothing against him now and hadn't then. When Jamey asked me. And I remember saying something like, 'Why don't you let it lie, sir?' and the obvious, meaningless bit about its not bringing Liz back."

126

"When was this?"

"Captain, I don't get—oh, all right. Maybe you do. A couple of weeks ago. And Jamey merely nodded his head, the way he often did, indicating that I had made a point and that he was aware of the point."

Bill Weigand looked at Mullins, who had been making notes.

"You've no idea who might've shot you?" Mullins said. "For the record?"

"No."

"And don't know anything you haven't told us about who might've killed the professor?"

"No."

"You realize—" Mullins began, and stopped and said, "O.K. Far's I'm concerned."

They both stood up, started toward the door of the hospital room. Bill Weigand stopped with his hand on the knob and turned back.

"By the way," he said. "The door from the Oldham house into the professor's laboratory. You know the door I mean?" Hunter moved his head affirmatively on the pillow. "You have a key to it?"

Hunter turned his head to look at Weigand. He said, "No. Why should I?" He considered Weigand for some seconds, his gray eyes intent. "You think somebody used that door?"

"I don't know," Bill said. "It's a possibility, of course. Who had keys? Elwell himself, I suppose. Miss Oldham says she had. Any others?"

He would, Hunter said, have to ask somebody else. But then he said, "Keys are a dime a dozen, you know. All you need is one to start with."

"Mrs. Oldham?"

"I don't know. I can't see her popping in on Jamey.

127

Or being asked to. But, I've no idea about the key. Why don't you ask her?"

"I shall," Bill said.

He turned back toward the door.

"Seems to me," the man on the bed said, "that there was something about—" But he stopped. He said no, he guessed not. Bill and Mullins waited. "No," Hunter said again. "If there was anything, it's gone. Probably wasn't."

"About the key?"

"That's what I thought for a moment. But if it was, it's gone."

Bill had his hand again on the doorknob. But again he turned back. There was one other thing. Hunter had arranged to pick Miss Oldham up for lunch? That was—Miss Oldham was expecting him?

"Sure," Hunter said. "That is—sure."

A standing arrangement? Or had he telephoned?

Not quite a standing arrangement. Rather, a common one. A "tomorrow the usual time?" sort of thing. And the answer, in this case, "yes."

In the car, Mullins started the motor, but did not shift into gear. He looked at Weigand, who waited.

"He wasn't much hurt," Mullins said. "Of course, most people can't hit anything with a revolver. But— And he couldn't have done it himself. But—And if the bullet matches, as it's gonna, Loot, he's sorta in the clear. And—the girl knew he'd be about there about then. And—that there was a cop pretty close and that cops are supposed to know something about first aid."

"Right," Bill said. "A little drastic but—could be."

"There's other things a helluva lot more drastic," Mullins said, and started the car rolling.

"On the other hand," Bill said, at the next stop light, "it would be nice to know what Hunter almost remembered."

"If anything," Mullins said, and got "Right, sergeant," and the light changed.

Mr. Arnold Ames had been rubbed to a high polish. He sat behind a desk which had been similarly treated. He was in his thirties—dark and handsome and, unless he had remarkably short legs, tall. He was a "realtor," flocking with others of his kind in a building to themselves in the near-east Fifties, where even small buildings are costly things. He looked across his desk at Bill Weigand. He said that he had been shocked to read of the death of Professor Elwell. He said that it was difficult to imagine such things happening to persons one knew, even slightly.

"Although," Ames said, "even that's an exaggeration. I met him once. Maybe twice."

"Through Miss Oldham?"

"Yes. Did Faith suggest you interview me? I can't imagine why she would have thought of such—" He concluded that with a shrug. His jacket, Bill thought, fitted beautifully.

Bill offered the usual, not always entirely convincing, explanations. In such things as this, all avenues must be explored; the most trivial relationships clarified. Miss Oldham had been, it was evident, a close friend of the professor. Mr. Ames might, conceivably, know some tiny thing—It did not sound especially convincing to Bill himself. But Ames nodded his head, the gesture dignified beyond his years.

"She did talk a good deal about Professor Elwell," he said. "Or Uncle Jamey, as she called him."

The tense was interesting. "Did?"

"Does still, I suppose," Ames said. "Or did until this happened. What I meant was, I haven't seen her for—oh, several weeks. So I can't understand why she—"

"Actually," Bill Weigand said. "It was her mother mentioned you, Mr. Ames."

Ames said, "Oh," and put the tips of his fingers together and looked over the steeple at Bill Weigand, as if estimating his reliability as a tenant. He said, "Oh," again. He said, "So she's been—being helpful." Then he said that it wasn't really any business of the police. He said it was, in fact, a little embarrassing. However—

"I met Faith last spring," he said. "Or late last winter. At some sort of party. She's an attractive girl, in an off-beat sort of way. Don't you think so?"

"Yes," Bill said.

"For one thing," Ames said, "she can make you feel like a protector. Not by anything she works at. Just by being the way she is. Actually, I doubt if she needs much protection. Don't you?"

"I've only met her," Bill said. "Asked some questions when she was under stress. No doubt you're right."

"And, it doesn't have anything to do with Professor Elwell's death."

"Probably not. However—"

"We went around together for a few weeks. Cocktails, dinner, dancing a little. Not precisely a thing, you understand, but something that could have got to be a thing. Maybe."

"And didn't because?"

"Mostly," Ames said, "because a man named

Hunter came along. He'd been around for some time, I gather, but all the same he—well, came along is good enough. Sort of thing they write songs about, I guess. Hasn't happened to me so far, but there you are."

It was not, at a guess, the sort of thing too likely to happen to Arnold Ames. But that was only a guess; the most polished surface may, presumably, cover great surging.

"It doesn't," Bill said, "seem to have upset you much."

"Now I don't know I—" Ames began, with surface slightly riffled. But then he said, "O.K. No, it didn't. Nice little thing. But there are a good many nice little things about, aren't there? Without mothers who—"

He stopped abruptly. And Bill waited.

"All right," Ames said. "Between us?"

"If it hasn't any bearing."

Weigand could be sure it hadn't. Between them, then—

"I said it was a little embarrassing," Ames said. "Well, Mrs. Oldham—Faith calls her Hope all the time—she—well, got notions. You know what I mean?"

"That there was more between you and Miss Oldham than there was?"

He could call it that. More than there was at the time, or was at all likely to be. "Although," Ames said, "I don't argue it was as clear to me then as it got to be later. Faith's a damn nice little thing. The thing was, we hadn't—" He paused again. "Put it this way," he said. "Mrs. Oldham jumped the gun by—by a hell of a long way. Probably there wouldn't ever have been a gun, even if Hunter hadn't showed up—across a crowded room, for all I know. And—well, that sort of thing makes a man shy off. Me, anyway. Especially when it's so damn clear—"

He looked at Bill with the expression of a man who has made it clear. Bill shook his head.

"All right," Ames said. "I said it was embarrassing. My family's got a bit of money. I've—oh, never been in jail. Or in the tabloids or—been notoriously feeble-minded or got myself into jams and that sort of thing. Gives mothers of pretty young daughters ideas, sometimes. Hell of a thing to have to explain, but there it is."

Bill said he saw. He said that it was evident, then, that "you and Miss Oldham don't —contemplate marriage."

"Never did," Ames said. "Could be it—what there was of it—was cooling a bit even before Hunter showed. And, Mrs. Oldham got—possessive. And got pretty obvious. And—"

Bill waited.

"All right," Ames said. "Took the edge off a bit. Also—how could I tell how much of—well, of Faith's seeming to take to me was Faith and how much mama? See what I mean?"

Bill saw. He said, "Mrs. Oldham has a good deal of influence over her daughter, you think?"

"A lot," Ames said. "Anyway, I thought so until—well, until Hunter showed up. Faith must have made a break then because—well, from all I hear, Hunter hasn't got any money. And mama—" He shrugged again.

Again Bill said he saw. There was one other point: During the time he had known Faith Oldham had Mr. Ames felt that Professor Elwell also had a good deal of influence over her? That she relied on him?

Ames said, "Well—" on a note of consideration. Then he nodded his head.

"She seemed to admire him a lot," he said. "Her own father had been dead since she was a child. And Elwell had, I gather, been kind and—well, I suppose he may have more or less taken her father's place. This is all guessing, you know. And it's not the sort of thing I know much about, or think much about. And I certainly can't see it has any bearing."

"Probably not," Bill said. "But—I'd better ask you this, Mr. Ames. Have you any reason to think that Professor Elwell may have influenced Miss Oldham in favor of Mr. Hunter? Hunter seems to be by way of having a protégé of Elwell's and—"

And Arnold Ames laughed across his polished desk. He laughed so heartily that two polished men at nearby polished desks looked at him in surprise, even, Bill Weigand thought, in reproof.

"Being a cop must be the damnedest thing," Ames said, when he had finished laughing. "Have to think of the damnedest things. Did Elwell alienate Faith's affections from me, to Hunter? And did I, surging with unrequited passion—for God's sake, captain!"

"We have," Bill said, "to look at all conceivable sides of a question, Mr. Ames."

He certainly did, Ames said. He sure as hell did, apparently.

"At three o'clock yesterday afternoon, captain," Ames said, "I was showing a charming couple through a charming apartment in the Sutton Place area—a very out of this world duplex, completely air-conditioned yet with wood-burning fireplaces and a view of the East River. From two-thirty until almost four. Charming couple will so depose and—" He shrugged under the perfectly fitting jacket.

"Good," Bill Weigand said. "Did you rent the apartment, Mr. Ames?"

Ames began to laugh again, and Bill thanked him and left him laughing. It seemed altogether probable that what Arnold Ames was having was the last laugh.

Driving back to West Twentieth Street, Bill nevertheless felt that he had been touched by the feathery suggestion of something. Whatever it was had, however, fluttered away. It was to be hoped it would, in time, flutter back. He would merely have to wait.

Pamela North returned to her apartment at around three-thirty, and was somewhat heavily laden, having stopped en route at the offices of North Books, Inc. She brought with her a copy of *Hypnotism in the Modern World*, by Jameson Elwell, Ph.D., Professor of Psychology at Dyckman University, a new cookbook, two mysteries and a volume of modern poetry, if here a distinction may be made. She riffled through the cookbook to see what was new, read one of the modern poems three times and settled with *Hypnotism in the Modern World*. Martini sat on her lap and, as time passed, was now and then read to.

"Listen to this, Teeney," Pam said. " 'The technics used in inducing hypnotism can, with practice, be learned by almost anyone. Neither a dominating personality nor a glittering eye is in any way essential.' Think of that, Teeney."

"Mrrr-ow-*oo!*"

"You may well say that," Pam said, and scratched Martini under the chin, at which Martini swished her tail.

Pam read further, only now and then sharing her discoveries with her cat. It was, she thought, odd that, while almost anybody—if Professor Elwell was right—could learn to hypnotize, only a rather small minority could learn to be hypnotized.

"Think of that," she said to Martini at one point, "a good operator can condition a good subject so that, after he has hypnotized him enough times, and reinforced a posthypnotic suggestion, all he has to do to put him back in hypnosis is to snap his fingers."

"Um-ow?" Martini said.

"The operator's fingers," Pam said. "You sound like Jerry."

She learned that—always assuming Jamey had known what he was talking about, which she was entirely ready to assume—a hypnotic subject may indeed be purged of all memory of any trance and may, further, be convinced that he is impervious to hypnotism. She read also that a good operator can make even the best subject insusceptible to being hypnotized by anyone else. She read a good deal, in small takes, using the thick volume as if it were Little Jack Horner's Christmas pie.

But what she sought, and what she did not find, was a flat statement that a person hypnotized could be directed to commit a major crime. She found "perhaps"; there was no dearth of "it-may-bes."

"The trouble with professors," Pam told Martini, "is that they qualify. If only they would come right out and say so. Or, of course, not so."

Martini did not reply, having fallen asleep. Conceivably, it occurred to Pam, into a hypnotic trance. There is not much she puts beyond Martini.

"You are falling sound asleep," Pam told Martini.

"Relax. You are falling sound asleep. Deeper and deeper asleep. Listen to me. You are falling sound asleep. Asleep, asleep—fast, fast asleep. Listen to me—"

"Mrrow-*ow*-oo," Martini said and got down and sat on the floor and looked at Pam. "Owr," Martini said, shortly. "Owr. Owr. OO-*row*."

It appeared not to work with cats. At any rate, not at what a cat regarded as dinner time. Martini went toward the kitchen. "Tell Martha," Pam said and Martini went on, telling Martha—and anybody else listening—with each step.

Pam returned to Elwell. Jerry had said he might be late; that he was sitting up with a sick manuscript. He was; it was almost six-thirty when he let himself in, and he said, "Wow!"—sounding rather like Martini. He said also that he was pooped and sat deeply in a chair and said, "Where is it?"

It was coming right up. It came up.

"Although of course," Pam said, sipping her own, "it isn't as good as when you make it."

"It's fine," Jerry said. "You can do them always."

"You do a kind deed," Pam said, "and it bounces back on you. You look tired."

"I am," Jerry said. "Parsons has only a smattering of English."

"But you say yourself he sells well."

"The connection," Jerry said, dreamily, "escapes me entirely." He then held out an empty glass. He was told he shouldn't gulp. He waggled the glass and Pam took it, and retired toward the bar. Jerry leaned his head back; closed his eyes.

"You are falling sound asleep," Pam said, tenderly,

from across the room. "Sound, sound asleep. Deeper and deeper asleep. You must relax completely. You are falling sound, sound asleep."

She paused. Had he not, visibly, relaxed? The chair, perhaps. Or, conceivably, the rapidly consumed martini. Surely not—

"Sound asleep," Pam said, more or less on momentum. "You are falling—"

She stopped herself, poured water out of the martini pitcher, put ice in, added other ingredients, stirred. There was the engaging rattle of ice within glass. She looked at Jerry. He certainly did look asleep. Which was, of course, nonsense.

She poured his drink into a freshly chilled glass. She twisted lemon rind, as she had been taught. She carried the glass across the room. And Jerry slept. She put it down on the table beside his chair, and put it down with a click louder than was called for. Jerry slept.

"Jerry?" Pam said.

He slept.

"Jerry?"

And nothing happened.

But this was absurd.

"Jerry!!"

Professor Elwell said, without qualification, that there was no need to fear that a hypnotized person would not awaken, when instructed. He said it emphatically.

"Wake up," Pam said. "Wake up, Jerry."

"Nice doggy," Jerry said. "Here, fella. Nice dog."

He reached down. He began to pat—*nothing*. But it was precisely as if—

"*Jerry!*" Pam said, and now there was a wail in it. "Jerry. *Darling*. Wake up. There isn't any dog. And I didn't—"

She stopped abruptly. He wouldn't be patting a non-existent dog unless she had—

"*You!*" Pam North said. "Of all the things—"

Jerry North opened his eyes.

"*You!*" Pam said.

She reached down. She picked up the martini from the table beside Jerry's chair and carried it to a table beside her own.

"You're strong enough," Pam said, firmly. "Make your own drink, my ever playful friend."

9

If I had gone on at Columbia, Bill Weigand thought, patiently, not happily, driving his Buick through the clotted traffic of late afternoon—if I were a lawyer now, it would be almost time to be leaving the office, going home. Or if I were an accountant, or an office manager—or, for that matter, a shoe salesman, a bookkeeper. I would be going toward home now, instead of away from it; toward Dorian instead of Sergeant Aloysius Mullins. I would be flicking the job off my hands, dusting it off, saying sufficient unto the day. There would be glasses chilling in the refrigerator, and Dorian curled waiting in a chair and all as right as right could—

On the other hand, Bill thought, stopping behind an out-of-town car which had, unexpectedly, decided to turn left—on the other hand, would I, if I had turned out to be—say—a shoe salesman, ever have met Dorian? Would she have come in to buy a pair of shoes and would we have gone on from there? It seemed somewhat doubtful. For one thing, as a shoe salesman—settle for that—it seemed unlikely he would have met Pamela and Gerald North, because what would it have mattered to him that they had found the body of a naked man in a bathtub? And if he had not met them, then how Dorian at that odd, attractive colony the Norths had frequented in other, earlier years?

And would I, Bill wondered, turning, finally, right into Twenty-first Street, have been contented as a nine-to-fiver, without a revolver in a shoulder holster—a revolver I haven't, actually, used in years? Without wondering whether—say—a man named Arnold Ames is really as amused as he seems to be; a man named Carl Hunter as straightforward? And, whether—say—it is really possible to arrange, by means of hypnosis, one's own death when one decides it is time to die and, dying, resolve a long-moot question?

Bill Weigand parked his car and climbed stairs to the squad room and nodded to Mullins, who got up from behind a desk, carrying papers, and followed into the cubbyhole which was Weigand's office at Homicide, Manhattan West.

"Ames thought it was all quite comical," Weigand told Mullins. "He may have been right. Do you bring in any choice sheaves? Oh—and did you remember to bring the professor's book along?"

Mullins had. He laid it, with every evidence of distaste, on the desk in front of Bill Weigand. He also said, briefly, what he thought that whole business was a lot of. "Now sergeant," Bill said. "Further?"

"Ballistics says yes," Mullins told him. "Same gun. Thirty-two Smith and Wesson. The professor's was a little nicked, on account of a rib, but there was enough. Hunter's was nice and clean. Of course, it figured."

It had. More than one .32 would have been superfluous.

"The Connecticut boys sent the dope along," Mullins said. "Nothing in it we didn't know, far's I can see."

The dope was a copy of an accident report—the report on the fatal accident of 26 April, resulting in the deaths of Elizabeth Elwell, 24; Ernest Bainbridge, 58, and Doris Bainbridge, spouse, 54. Weigand skimmed through it and put it on the desk.

The lawyer of the late Jameson Elwell confirmed—after some legal hemming, and ethical hawing—that the provisions of his client's will were as stated by the decedent's brother. In all that was important. After thises and thats, residue in equal shares to two nephews, a niece, and Faith Oldham, spinster. The will was dated two months earlier; it superseded a testament of some years' standing, in which Faith Oldham was not mentioned.

"Looks," Mullins said, "as if he had seen a doctor, don't it?"

It suggested that. It need not prove that. Wills are changed otherwise than in the immediate expectation of death.

"Sure," Mullins said. "So I went to see Miss Oldham and her mother. Want to read about it or—?"

"Tell me, sergeant," Mullins's official reports are sometimes a little rigid.

"The girl says she was at the house," Mullins said. "Waiting for her boyfriend to show and take her out to lunch. Mrs. Oldham wasn't. She—"

Mrs. Oldham had left the house at about a quarter

141

after eleven to do the marketing. "Somebody has to," she said, and looked at her daughter, who sighed slightly, as one who encounters a too-familiar remark. "Somebody has to do the errands," Mrs. Oldham said, in case she had left doubt in the mind of Sergeant Mullins. Mullins said, "Yes'm."

She had not, walking up the street in the direction of Broadway, seen "that" Mr. Hunter. She had gone to a chain store and carried groceries home. "Somebody has to," she said. "They don't deliver for nothing, whatever they pretend. It just gets added on."

"She's not a very nice woman," Mullins said, in parenthesis, to Bill Weigand. "Way she looked at the girl, I mean."

Faith had got home a little after noon. When some time later, Carl Hunter had failed to arrive, she had first called his apartment and, getting no answer, gone to the front door and looked up and down the street. The patrolman still on guard outside the house next door had come down the street and said good morning and then, "Man just got shot up the street, miss," which was the first she had known of it. When she found out who the man was she had gone to the hospital. Hunter was still in surgery and she had waited until he came out of it—until he regained consciousness and could smile at her; until she had been told, several times, that he was not badly hurt.

Her mother had returned when Faith got home and said, on being told what happened, "I never did trust that Mr. Hunter. And your rushing off to the hospital that way!"

"That," Mullins said, "is what she said she said. And the girl said, 'Oh, *Hope*.' "

Mullins had said that his questions were formalities

to be gone through; that in such cases as this there were a lot of forms to fill out. "Which," he said, a little moodily, "God knows there are, Loot." With the formalities observed, he had stood and then said, "Oh, by the way. Congratulations on the silver lining, Miss Oldham."

They had both, he told Bill Weigand, stared at him as if he had gone out of his mind.

"The inheritance," Mullins said and, when they continued to stare, "in the professor's will."

Faith Oldham had shaken her head, then, and looked at her mother. Then they had both looked at Mullins and both had shaken their heads.

Now Bill Weigand raised his eyebrows.

"I think they were leveling," Mullins said. "Or they both oughta be on the stage. Which makes it interesting, doesn't it? Because if the girl didn't know, then Hunter didn't know and—well, there we are."

"You told them?"

Mullins had. It was no secret, or wouldn't long be.

"From the way they acted," Mullins said, "I'd say it pretty much knocked them over. Particularly Mrs. Oldham; particularly at first. Then she came out of it enough to say something about its being the least he could do. And the girl—she started to cry and said 'Hope!', all broken up like, and went out of the room. Makes you feel sorta sorry for the girl. If she didn't kill him, of course."

"Right," Bill said. "If she didn't kill him. And—if she didn't know about the money, she didn't have a motive, did she? Unless—"

"Listen, Loot," Mullins said. "Not that hypnotism stuff."

"And if she didn't have one," Weigand said,

143

"Hunter didn't and mama didn't. Unless Elwell—" He did not finish.

"Looks like it," Mullins said. "Be nice if it was mama. What I mean is—"

"I know," Bill Weigand said. "We must avoid prejudice, sergeant. Have the boys finished in the laboratory? Elwell's office?"

They had finished—that was, they had removed from laboratory and office all that they thought might conceivably be of value. They were going over it elsewhere. So far they hadn't found anything that looked like being anything, except for the payments to Investigators, Inc., of which they already knew.

"The trouble with us," Mullins said, "is that nobody ever leaves us any clues."

"I know," Weigand said. "If they've finished there we may as well put this with the rest of the stuff."

This tinkled on the desktop. This was the key to the laboratory which Weigand had taken from Faith Oldham the day before. Mullins, custodian of physical objects, picked it up and looked at it and started to clip it to a sheaf of papers and looked at it again.

"Looks new," Mullins said, and Bill Weigand reached for it. It did look new. Bill ran a finger along the wards. The sharpness of the cutting had not yet worn smooth.

"We were talking about the key when Hunter almost remembered something," Mullins said, but Weigand had already reached for the telephone. He told the operator whom he wanted to talk to, and where the wanted man was. "Of course," he said, as he put the telephone back, "what he almost remembered may have been about something entirely different."

They smoked and waited. The telephone rang. A

woman was saying that Mr. Hunter was under partial sedation and should not be disturbed, and then a man said, "Let me have it, please," Hunter's voice was, Bill thought, a little muted, as if Hunter were a little groggy. Bill said he wanted to ask only one thing, but that if Hunter didn't feel up to it—

"In a few minutes," Huner said, "I'll probably be asleep. So—what?"

"The thing you almost remembered when we were up there," Bill said. "Was it about the key to the professor's lab? About a key having been lost, perhaps, and another one made and—"

"Hell," Hunter said, and his voice was fading, "I don't even know if it was that. Could have been—wait a minute. Faith lost her key two-three weeks ago. She was standing over a subway grating and took something out of her purse—tissue, probably—and the key came out too and dropped through the grating."

"Was that what you remembered? Almost remembered."

"I don't know," Hunter said. "Seems to me that there was somthing more. Something—relevant. That losing the key was only—" Then there was a long pause. "Maybe when this stuff they've given me wears off—" Hunter said, and his voice was vague. And then a woman said, "Mr. Hunter must be allowed to rest now," and put a receiver back in a hospital room. Weigand put his back, and told Mullins what Hunter had said.

"So all it means, probably," Bill said, "is that Miss Oldham borrowed the professor's key long enough to have another made. Which doesn't seem—"

He stopped. He drummed briefly on the desktop with his fingers. He said, "Let me have that a minute," but, when Mullins started to hand him the key, "No. The accident report."

Weigand flicked back the first page of the stapled two-page report. He read what he had previously skimmed. He said, "Un-huh" and, "Listen to this, sergeant," and read:

" 'Small evening purse on seat of car; gray silk with metal clasp. Contents: compact, lipstick, handkerchief initialed EE, coin purse containing single five-dollar bill, vial of perfume (Arpege), driver's license No. 5280846, NY, made out to Elizabeth Elwell, Age 24—' "

"And," Bill said, "etcetera. What's missing, sergeant?"

"Cigarettes," Mullins said, promptly. "Lighter. Social security card."

"I don't know she was employed," Bill said. "Or would carry a card in an evening purse if she were. And cigarettes and lighter might be pretty bulky for an evening purse. Particularly when you're with a man who has pockets. Anything else?"

"I don't—" Mullins said, and tapped the desktop with clenched fist, self-punishing. "What we were just talking about," he said. "Keys."

"Right," Bill said. "For everybody there's a door some place."

"Well," Mullins said, "not everybody."

"Everybody who might conceivably drive a Jaguar," Bill said. "To one's own front door, sergeant."

"Looks," Mullins said, "like we'd better go and talk to this Mr. Flinch.". . .

Rosco Finch was about to go out to dinner. He had a date for dinner. Also, he had told them everything—

"Told you," he said to Mullins. "I don't know who hired those detectives. And, I don't give a damn. It's all water under—"

He stopped and looked at Bill Weigand through narrowed eyes. He said, "Wait a minute," and then, "You say your name's Weigand?"

Bill had. He nodded his head.

"You're Homicide," Finch said, and spoke accusingly. "And Professor Elwell's been murdered." He turned on Mullins. "Which," he said, "you were damn careful not to tell me, weren't you?"

"Yes," Mullins said.

"So all this business about the accident," Finch said. "About checking up on this private detective. A lot of hogwash."

"Look here, mister," Mullins said, but Bill Weigand cut through.

"Not entirely, Mr. Finch," Bill said. "We're a good deal interested in the private detective who came to talk to you about the accident. Because—Professor Elwell hired him, Mr. Finch."

Finch said, "What the hell?" in a tone of great surprise.

"No," Bill said. "I think you knew. Or—guessed. Well?"

"I told the sergeant—"

"I know what you told the sergeant. I think you guessed if you didn't know. Well?"

"What difference does it make? I didn't know. I'll admit I—wondered."

"And," Bill said, "wondered if maybe they'd found out more than they told you. About the accident. That you *were* driving and—"

"They couldn't have," Finch said. "Because I wasn't. And—I don't have to tell you a damn thing more, do I?"

He was belligerent.

"Not a thing," Bill Weigand said, with no belligerence at all. "All right, Mullins. We'll take him along. Book him and—"

"Book me? For what?"

The belligerence remained, even increased. And sounded—Bill hoped it sounded—a little hollow.

"Material witness," Bill said. Covers a multitude of sins, Mr. Finch. And—possibilities. Material witness in connection with the murder of Professor Jameson Elwell. And then you won't have to answer my questions. Anyway, not only mine. There'll be a man from the D.A.'s office and—"

"I tell you," Finch said, "I wasn't driving. Nobody can prove I was driving."

"That," Bill said, "is what you hope. Could be, this man Flanagan would have a different story. Could be he passed it on to the professor and the professor gave you a chance to prove Flanagan wrong before he got the case reopened and—"

"You'll never," Finch said, "make that stick. Anyway—who'd kill anybody for as little reason as that? Suppose I *was* driving. It was still an accident. Suppose something went wrong with the steering and—"

"Suppose," Bill said, "you had been drinking and fell asleep at the wheel. Doing eighty. Suppose it's held vehicular homicide. You'd get a stretch for that, Mr. Finch. Wouldn't be much of a golfer when you got out, probably."

Finch had been standing, as Bill Weigand and Mullins had. Now, suddenly, he sat down. They looked down at him.

"Damn it all," he said. "Liz was—" He stopped and pressed his forehead with the palms of his hands. "She was dead," he said. "There wasn't anything more could happen to—hurt her. And—" He seemed to catch himself. "She was driving the car," he said, his tone flat, final. "She wanted to and I let her. Just as I told the police then. And nobody can—"

"Prove," Bill said. "Perhaps not. It's hard to know about that though, isn't it? And this stirring things up—"

"I've told you all I'm going to," Finch said. "All there is to tell."

There is no use pressing too long on precisely the same spot.

"Miss Elwell had a purse," Bill said. "A gray silk evening purse. It was found in the car. Mr. Finch—did you take anything out of that purse?"

Finch stood up again, abruptly. He said, "Damn it all! Now you want to make me out a thief?"

"Did you take anything out of the purse?"

"I didn't touch the purse. And if you—"

"Mister," Sergeant Mullins said, "why don't you just sit down? Take it easy, sort of?"

Mullins looked heavily at Rosco Finch. And Finch sat down.

"I didn't touch the purse," Finch said again. "Something missing from the purse?"

"I don't know," Bill said. "I'd think so. Finch, did you take a key—perhaps several keys in a holder of some sort—out of Miss Elwell's purse? Did you—use one of the keys yesterday? At about three o'clock? The key to the Elwell front door?"

"I—" Finch began. But there was no belligerence left now.

"Don't," Bill told him, "tell me you were at the golf club practicing drives. We've checked on that. Nobody saw you there. And—there were people about who would have. So—"

Bill waited. Sometimes you took chances; sometimes tried a bluff. And sometimes the bluff was called.

"I didn't take the keys," Finch said. "What would I want to steal keys for? She didn't have room in the bag and—"

He stopped.

"What the hell?" he said. "What the hell?"

He seemed to speak in bewilderment, in discouraged wonder at mischance. They waited, saying nothing.

"All right," he said. "She gave me the keys to carry, because they made a bulge with all the other things she carried in her purse. You know how they are about that?"

"Right," Bill said. "She gave you the keys."

"Will you let me tell it?" Finch said. "It's not so good, but let me tell it. Because I didn't kill Elwell. And I wasn't driving the car. I'll stick to that, captain."

"Right," Bill said. "You'll stick to that. Stick to both of them."

"I didn't kill Elwell. Suppose you give me a chance to tell it."

"The sergeant will make notes," Bill said. "When we get in we'll type it up. And, as I said, you don't have to—"

"Sure," Finch said, and the belligerence came back.

"You badger me and this sergeant can push me around and—"

"Nobody's pushed you around," Bill said. "Do you want to tell us about the keys?"

"I'll be—" Finch began, and then the belligerence drained out. "What's the use?" Finch said dully, and seemed to speak to himself. "I—"

He had, he said, been dazed after the accident, partly from shock, partly because he had got a bang on the head. He had forgotten all about the keys at the time, thought of them later and put them in a drawer, forgotten them again in the confusion of other things. "They kept badgering me," he said. "Nobody asked me about the keys and what had they to do with it, anyway? Believe me or don't believe me, I forgot all about them."

The whole accident had begun to be dim in his mind—"and thank God for that"—and then Flanagan appeared and brought it back. And then—

"All right," he said. "I thought maybe Liz's father was back of it. I didn't know. I just thought he might be. And then I did remember the keys. So—"

The keys gave an excuse, Finch said. He would go around to see Professor Elwell, ostensibly to return the keys and to apologize for not having returned them months ago. And—if he could talk to Elwell he could, he thought, tell whether Elwell was back of Flanagan, and had sent Flanagan.

"And," Finch said, "find out just where I stood. I wasn't going to bring it up in so many words unless I had to. But if it turned out he didn't believe she was driving—I thought maybe I could convince him. Because—well, after Flanagan began nosing around, I nosed around a little myself and—all right, found out about this vehicular homicide. As I say, I wasn't driving but—well, it was my car and the way it happened—what it comes down to, nobody can prove I was driving but I don't know any way I can prove I wasn't and—"

"Mr. Finch," Bill said. "I'm not a Connecticut policeman. Unless it ties in with Professor Elwell's death, what happened last April isn't any official business of mine. Were you driving?"

Finch hesitated for a moment before answering; looked up at Weigand with slightly narrowed eyes. But when he did answer it was to repeat, with again a moment of truculence, that Liz Elwell had been at the Jaguar's wheel.

Bill shrugged his shoulders at that. He said, "You decided to see the professor, ostensibly to return the keys. And—got around to it yesterday."

"I didn't say—" Finch was silent for several seconds. "I suppose somebody saw me," he said.

So that was that. And they might, of course, eventually find somebody who had seen Rosco Finch.

"Go ahead," Bill said. "You went to the house. Used the key, probably, and—"

Again he was invited to let Finch tell it. All right, Finch had gone to the house. Some time around three. And—

"Hold it a minute," Mullins said. "When I was here before you already knew Elwell was dead. *And* had this story about practicing golf ready and—"

"All right," Finch said. "It was on the radio. And nobody wants to get mixed up in things if he can help it."

Which was true enough of most people; which was obviously very true of Finch.

"Go ahead," Weigand said. "We'll pick up the pieces later, sergeant," and Mullins said, "O.K., Loot-I-mean-captain."

"If you mean," Finch said, "did I just use the key and walk in, no, I didn't. I rang the doorbell, and waited and rang it again and was just about to give it up when—"

When, from somewhere inside the house, he had heard what sounded like a shot. It had sounded distant, muffled; he had not been sure that it was a shot. But he also was not sure it wasn't and, instead of going away as he had been about to do, he rang the doorbell again—rang it several times. And it was still unanswered.

"Hell," Finch said, "I liked the old guy. Whatever you think, captain. I liked him. And I thought—maybe he was cleaning a gun or something and alone in the house and had managed to shoot himself and needed help. So—"

So he had got out the leather container of keys. There were half a dozen, and three of them of the type which might fit the lock of the door he faced. He tried them in order, and tried wrong twice. Inside, when the last of the three worked, he had at first called out, and then, being unanswered, begun to look into various rooms, in search of a wounded man. And he had, reasonably enough, started on the first floor.

So it had been at least five minutes after he heard the shot—and perhaps more than five minutes—that he had found Elwell dead at his desk.

"You knew he was dead?"

Anybody would have known that. And—Finch had been a hospital corpsman in the navy during the Korean fighting, and had had plenty of opportunity to learn the look of death.

"If there had been anything I could have done," Finch said, "I'd have tried it. If there'd been anything *any*body could have done, I'd—I'd have called for help. Believe me or—"

He ended with a shrug which said he supposed they wouldn't believe it and that there was no use arguing.

"O.K.," he said. "When there wasn't anything I could do, I got out. I didn't want to be mixed up in anything if I could help it. And, considering the accident and everything, I realized it wouldn't—" He shrugged again.

"Look so good," Bill said. "Right. You lit out. Taking the keys with you?"

He had. And now, unprompted, he reached into his jacket pocket and took out a leather key container and, mutely, held it out. It did contain six keys; three of them were for locks of similar type. Which didn't prove anything one way or another. Bill gave the keys to Mullins, who put them in a pocket.

Rosco Finch sat and looked at them and there was speculation in his eyes and uneasiness.

"Do you own a gun?" Bill asked him and he shook his head slowly from side to side. "So," Bill said, "you couldn't have carried one with you when you went to see Professor Elwell."

Finch did not answer that, in word or movement. He kept on looking at Bill Weigand.

"How did you get to the house?"

He had gone there in a cab. What kind of cab? One of the little ones, the ones hard to get into. A name on the cab? He didn't remember any. Its color? Yellow, he thought; or yellow and black. Or maybe yellow and red.

"Be fair, captain," Finch said. "Do you pay attention to what kind of cab you get into? Note down the name of the driver and his number? Most people don't."

Which was, of course, entirely true. And it was also true that, while time and men could turn up a cab whose trip record showed a stop outside the Elwell house, the time would be long and the men numerous. And, probably, nothing proved, except an approximate time of arrival.

"Describe the way you found the professor. And the room."

Finch did. He had been there.

"There's a closet door," Bill said. "Remember it?"

Finch rubbed his chin. He remembered another door, roughly opposite the door he had entered by. Was it open or closed?

"I'd have noticed if it had been open," Finch said. "So it must have been closed. You mean—somebody could have been hiding in a closet?"

Which might mean that Finch thought it really was a closet, not a passageway, or that Finch was lying about it—or that, in fact, the second entrance to the room had nothing to do with anything.

"After you heard the shot," Bill Weigand said. "Before you decided to use a key and go in and investigate, I take it nobody came out of the house? Came past you?"

"For God's sake," Finch said, reasonably enough. "And said, 'Afternoon. By the way, I just killed Professor Elwell'? For God's sake, captain."

"And," Bill said, "you didn't find anybody in the house? Anybody alive?"

Finch merely looked at him, and shook his head in wonder at such obviousness. But then he said, "I suppose there's a back door, captain? And—there was time enough."

"All right," Bill said. "Do you know a man named Hunter? Carl Hunter?"

Finch had met him a few times, at Elwell's house. Knew he was working with Elwell. "Something about cats," Finch said. "God knows why."

Mullins looked at Finch, momentarily, with something like sympathy.

"What they called an egghead," Finch said. "Like the professor himself. Psychiatrist, or something like that."

"Psychologist," Bill said, absently. "You didn't see Mr. Hunter yesterday?"

Finch said, "Huh?"

"At the Elwell house," Bill said. "Going away from the house."

"No. Was he there?"

The idea obviously somewhat brightened Finch's darkening mood. The question did not, however, get an answer.

"Do you know a Miss Faith Oldham?"

"Tall, skinny girl? I met her once, I think. Hey—seems to me Liz once said something about Hunter and the girl being—that way. Only there was something about another man and—" He stopped, evidently feeling that he had strayed, or been enticed, from the point. He looked at Weigand with renewed suspicion.

"You didn't see her at the house yesterday? Or near it?"

"I didn't see anybody at the house."

"About eleven-thirty this morning," Weigand said. "Where were you then, Mr. Finch?"

"I don't—" Finch began.

"Never mind. Where were you?"

Finch had left some "gear" at the club in Connecticut. He had driven up to get it and, at eleven-thirty, he was somewhere between the club and his apartment, driving back. Alone? Yes, he had been alone.

"Something happened then?" Finch said.

"Mr. Hunter got shot," Bill said. "Shot and wounded, but not badly. So, it looks as if he might have seen something, or might know something, doesn't it?"

Finch didn't know what it looked like. All he knew was that Elwell had been dead when he found him, and was it an offense to go away, knowing him dead? "Whatever you think about it," Finch added, and tried to make his voice hard and only partly succeeded.

"Yes," Bill said. "It is. I can take you in on that. Or as a witness. Or, on a charge of suspicion of homicide."

"So?"

"For the moment, I'm going to tell you not to leave the city. And—take steps to see you don't. Go keep your dinner date, Mr. Finch—if it's in town.". . .

"Why?" Mullins said, when they were back in the car. "Could be we've got enough. He had a grudge, or could have had. He was there. He—"

"Right," Bill said. "And the D.A. wouldn't buy it. And if he bought it, a grand jury wouldn't. And if a grand jury did, a trial jury wouldn't. Yet. If we could prove he was driving the car. But we can't, and I doubt if we're going to be able to."

"He was," Mullins said. "It sticks out."

Bill nodded his head to that. It stuck out. It didn't make Finch a particularly responsible citizen, or a particularly desirable one. But neither did it make him a murderer, at least of Jameson Elwell.

Mullins started the car. He said he supposed Bill was right.

"He'd be too easy," Mullins said. "Screwy, but not screwy enough. With the Norths in it? We try the other keys, I suppose?"

They did. One of the keys fitted the door of the house the Oldhams lived in. One of them fitted the door from that house to the laboratory. The third of the almost identical group fitted the lock of the front door of the Elwell house.

Bill Weigand dropped Mullins at a subway station and drove home, through diminished traffic. It would, he thought, be nice to come up with a hunch. Or, for that matter, evidence. It would be nice to know whether Faith Oldham and her mother had lied when they denied knowing of Faith's inheritance. If they had, both the girl and Hunter would have had motives—the mother, too, for that matter. It would be nice to *know*— rather than only to suspect strongly— that Finch had been driving the Jaguar months ago. It would be interesting to know whether Elwell had used his influence over Faith to persuade her that Hunter was preferable to the polished and affluent Arnold Ames. It would be nice to know whether a person could be, under hypnosis, persuaded to kill.

It would be nice to have a hunch.

10

After dinner, Jerry North read manuscript, shuddering from time to time. Pam North read Jameson Elwell on hypnotism, at intervals saying, "Jerry! It says here—" To which Gerald North said, for the most part, "Um-m-m," and now and then, "You ought to see what it says *here,* for God's sake." Reading Elwell on hypnotism turned out, Pam found, to be more like eating peanuts than, as she had first supposed, plumbing a Christmas cake. As the evening progressed, she learned to skip over those passages in which technics were stressed—"you are growing sleepy; you are falling into a deep sleep," for example—to avoid autosuggestion.

"You don't talk in your sleep much," Pam said, at one point, and Jerry said, "Um-m-m," and then, hearing her, "Huh?"

"Which probably explains it," Pam said, and got a more emphatic "Huh?" "Your not responding earlier," Pam said, and at this Jerry laid down the manuscript and invited Pam to come again.

"When I pretended to try to hypnotize you," Pam said, "and you pretended I had. Cad, incidentally, while I think of it. People who talk in their sleep are usually good subjects, and if they will let you talk back without waking up, they're even better. That's what it says here. And those who actually get up and walk around in their sleep are the best of all."

"This man," Jerry said, and tapped the manuscript—"this man talks in my sleep. What does that mean?"

"I haven't come across that yet," Pam said, and then, "If you're not interested. Martini—it says here that all animals can be hypnotized. Teeney!"

Martini flicked the extreme tip of her tail.

"You," Pam said, to Martini, "are falling fast asleep. Fast, fast asleep."

Which was true enough.

"Only," Jerry pointed out, "she was already."

But this time it was Pam who said "um-m-m," having found another peanut. Jerry watched Pam for a moment, always, to him, a satisfying activity, even when she is not doing anything. Then, with a sigh, he returned to duty. If only something would happen to somebody. Jerry was not particular what; he realized he was reading a modern novel and made no great demands. Any little thing. He would be satisfied if the hero, if he could be called that, would trip on something and fall downstairs. Or upstairs. Or, if that was too much to ask, catch a bad cold. Or even a slight cold. Anything to dam the stream of his consciousness.

It was getting so, Jerry thought, that there are only two kinds, and both of them long. Nobody will buy them any more unless they're long. Fiction goes by the pound, Jerry thought. Often enough, a pound of flesh. That is one kind—the sexual mechanics kind; the "let-me-tell-you-how-it-happens" kind, the telling each time with a fervor suitable to the newly discovered. That kind was, commonly, written by the middle-aged who would, one would have supposed, long since have lost the wide-eyed enthusiasm of puberty. But they had not, and, which was of more immediate importance to publishers, the reading public had not either. There was the other kind, and this—this which was, it had to be admitted, not completely holding his present attention—was of its species. In such, nothing whatever happened, including the obvious. And how the reviewers loved them. The trouble with me, Jerry thought, is that I've had a long day—a day with too many words in it. So I'm not being fair to "this" and—

"Jerry," Pam said, "it says here—"

She waited. He came up, and now thankfully.

What it said there was that people did not—unlike modern novels—come in two kinds. They were not—

"—not just hypnotists or hypnotees," Pam said. "One person can be both. He—Elwell, I'm talking about—"

"I know who you're talking about," Jerry said.

"Whom," Pam said. "He stresses that to prove it isn't a question of dominant will power. He says—I'll read you what he says—'The belief that the operator is a person of dominating will and the subject one easily dominated is, of course, without validity, being one of the superstitions which have clustered immemorially about the science in the popular mind.' He does write like a professor, doesn't he?"

"A little," Jerry admitted. "I especially like the 'of course,' don't you? Like the Russian 'as is well known.' Anticipatory reinforcement of the improbable, it's called."

"Is it?"

"As of the moment," Jerry said. "By me, anyhow."

"Let's stay on the subject," Pam said. "Anticipatory reinforcements of the improbable another time. All right? Anyway, he goes on—no, I'll translate as I go—he cites several cases in his own experience in which a single person was both an excellent subject for hypnotism and an experienced operator. By operator, he means 'hypnotist.' "

Jerry knew. He had, after all, read the book. Since he had—

"Published it," Pam said. "I know. Anyway, I know what you say. Then, you remember his case history? In this connection?"

Jerry did not contend that he remembered, in exact detail, each of the many case histories used for exemplification in the numerous pages of *Hypnotism in the Modern World*.

"About," Pam said, "a Mr. H. A young assistant of Jamey's in experiments; a man who was not only a good hypnotee but a good hypnotist—one of the best of each Jamey had ever encountered, although by no means unique in—'in having this dichotomous character.' Phew!"

"Phew indeed."

" 'Mr. H.' " Pam repeated. " 'H' for 'Hunter,' wouldn't you think?"

It was quite possible.

"A man of unusual intelligence and strength of character, Jamey says 'Mr. H.' is—was. In this field, as in others, a man uncommon not only in the discernment of his approach to the fields of research, but in the persistence and inventiveness with which he meets the problems of technic which so constantly arise in the science of psychology as, of course, in other sciences. I was reading that."

"I thought," Jerry said, "that I detected a somewhat different style."

"Mr. Hunter," Pam said. "Persistent. And—inventive."

"If," Jerry said, "a touch posthypnotic."

He was invited to be serious. He said by all means. Carl Hunter was persistent and inventive, in the judgment of a man who should have known; who was trained to know. And, where did it get them? In, as he supposed was the point, the question of the murder of Jameson Elwell, Ph.D.?

"I don't know," Pam said. And then she closed *Hypnotism in the Modern World.* "For all we know, Bill's solved it already. Is it too late to call up and ask him? After all, Jamey was your author."

It was, Jerry thought, a somewhat tenuous "after all." Furthermore, it was almost eleven o'clock.

"I suppose you're right," Pam said, without enthusiasm, and the door chimes sounded. "Now who ever at this hour?" Pam said, and went to see.

A slight woman in a close-fitting woolen dress stood at the door; a woman young of body, much less young of face; a woman with very brown hair and somewhat light blue eyes. She wore a beige fall coat and carried a black handbag under her left arm.

"Is Faith here?" the woman said. The voice was thin.

There was, inescapably, a moment of confusion. The Norths live in downtown Manhattan, where mankind still is variable. (Although not, residents of the area will tell you, wistfully, in the old way.) There are variables who offer tracts.

"Yes," Pam said, adopting the method experience had proved the most efficacious. "We are both saved."

This usually resulted in a "Bless you, sister," or even, now and again, in a "Hallelujah!" and, eventually, in departure, in most cases after the purchase, for a modest sum, of a tract.

"I don't—" the slight little woman said. "Oh—you are Mrs. North?" Pam nodded. "You didn't understand me," the little woman said. "Faith *Oldham*. My daughter. Is she here?"

Now Pam noticed that the thin voice was also a strained voice; that there was an odd intentness in the light blue eyes.

"No," Pam said. "But come in, Mrs. Oldham. Perhaps we—"

Hope Oldham did not wait for Pam to finish. She came into the room and looked around it, quickly, as if she had not believed denial, thought to see her daughter. But then, it seemed blindly, she groped for a chair and sat in it, and put her hands over her face.

"I so hoped—" she said. "I'm—so afraid something—"

The woman's slim body, which seemed to parody youth, began to shake as if mind had lost all control of trembling nerves. Pam went to her quickly, bent over the chair and put an arm around the shaking shoulders, holding the older woman close. "I'll be all right," Hope Oldham said, and said it again, in a voice which was not "all right."

She was crying—sobbing, at any rate. She was close to hysteria, Pam thought, holding her and making small meaningless sounds intended to bring comfort. And at the same time, apropos of nothing, uninvited, a thought edged into Pam North's mind. Those subject to hysteria are, "notoriously"—the word was Professor Elwell's—subject also to hypnosis. What had that to do with anything? "There," Pam said to Hope Oldham. "There. There." And again, the frail woman said she would be all right.

"Take a deep breath," Pam said. "A really deep breath."

Hope Oldham's breast—a younger woman's breast—rose as she breathed deeply. And her shoulders did not shake so under Pam's comforting, reassuring, arm. Again Hope drew air slowly, deeply, into her lungs.

"I'm all right now," she said, and this time the tone was different, this time the words had meaning. Pam released her and Hope Oldham managed a smile and said, "Thank you, my dear. It was just—" She stopped and again drew a deep breath.

"I so hoped she would be here," Mrs. Oldham said. "Was almost certain. To find she isn't—"

She seemed about to begin shaking again.

"Wait," Pam said. "We'll get you something. Coffee? Or—"

"Here," Jerry said, and held a small glass out. "Maybe this will help, Mrs. Oldham." She looked at it. "Cognac," Jerry said. "It'll be good for you."

She took it doubtfully. But she sipped from it and nodded her head over it.

"We'll all have—" Pam began, but Jerry had thought of that, also. They all had.

"I—"Mrs. Oldham began and Jerry, his voice very

gentle, said, "Finish it first." She finished. "Now," Jerry said. "Your daughter is—she's gone some place? You're trying to find her?"

"I thought she had come here," Mrs. Oldham said, and now her voice was reasonably steady. "I know I should have telephoned. Not just—forced my way in on you. At this hour, too. But I was so certain. I said to myself, 'Of course! That's it. Mrs. North was so kind earlier, so understanding, and now—of course she's gone there.' It was as if something *told* me. And—"

She stopped suddenly.

"She *was* here this morning?" Mrs. Oldham said, and spoke very quickly, with a return of excitement. "It wasn't just something she—told me? To throw me off the track?"

"She was here," Pam said. "To—" It was Pam's turn to stop, to consider. To find out, through her, what the police thought, specifically about Carl Hunter? That was, Pam supposed, the answer. (Although there might, of course, have been more to it.) "She just wanted somebody to talk to," Pam said. "She's so upset about Jamey and—"

"But not," Mrs. Oldham said, "not her own *mother*. Somebody she hardly knew at all!"

Which was certainly true.

"Well," Pam said.

"Sometimes," Jerry said, his voice still gentle, "sometimes it's easier to talk to people one isn't close to, Mrs. Oldham. One feels freer. With no past associations to—intervene."

"Her own *mother*," Mrs. Oldham said, as if she had not heard. "The poor, poor child. What have they done to her, Mrs. North? What have they *done* to her?"

She seemed to be working herself back into the mood of near hysteria. Certainly she was proceeding in anything but a straight line.

"Who?" Pam North said, seeking to direct traffic. "Who do you think has done something to her?"

"And for that matter," Jerry said, "done what?"

Now she looked at both of them, first at Pam, then at Jerry. Her eyes were very light blue; they did not hold tears. Her sobs, then, must have been part of a kind of nervous chill. She had not really been weeping. Probably it would be better for her if she could. But—about what?

"I'm sorry," Mrs. Oldham said. "It's the shock of— of realizing. I'm afraid I'm not very coherent. But—"

And then she started to get up from the chair.

"I'm terribly sorry to have barged in this way," she said, the idiom contemporary, the tone unexpectedly formal. "So late in the evening. Bothering you with things which can't possibly interest you, really. Although you have been very kind. *Very* kind. Since Faith isn't here—"

"Mrs. Oldham," Pam said, "if there's anything we can do to help." The young-old woman hesitated. "Look," Pam said. "Your daughter's gone away somewhere and you don't know where. You're worked up. But probably nothing's happened to her. Of *course* nothing's happened to her."

Pam got assurance into her clear voice; spoke as if she knew.

"It isn't—" Mrs. Oldham said, but then let herself sink back into the chair. "I do feel you want to help. Both of you."

167

"You speak," Jerry said, "as if something violent had happened. As if your daughter had been—*taken* away. But you surely didn't think we—we had done anything to *make* her come here?"

"Like," Pam North said, to her own surprise, "dragging her by the hair?"

Mrs. Oldham did not appear to hear that, which was probably as well. She said, to Jerry, that she hadn't meant that, of course, and that he didn't understand.

"I don't," Jerry said. "If there's any way we can help. But we'll have to know, first, what's happened."

They would, of course, think she was only a foolishly worried woman. She realized that. Anybody would think that who didn't—well, really know how things were. Because on the surface nothing had "happened" except that Faith Oldham had got a telephone call and, afterward, gone out without telling her mother where she was going.

"As if," Hope Oldham said, "she didn't *trust* me. And, didn't care how much I worried."

"Well," Pam said, "she isn't exactly a child, Mrs. Oldham. It's more considerate to tell people where you're going, of course, but one can't always." Her remark started a faint echo in Pam's echo-prone mind. Of course, "after every meal." It is pleasant to settle such things as one goes along.

"For all you know, then," Jerry said, and he was very calm. "For all you know some friend called her and said, come over for a drink. Or a cup of coffee. And you weren't around and—"

Mrs. Oldham was shaking her head from side to side. She had been around.

She had, to be sure, been in the tub. This had

been—oh, about ten. "I always take a hot bath before I go to bed," Mrs. Oldham said. "It makes it so much easier to sleep. Because of course I never take anything."

Pam nodded her head, acknowledging the rectitude of that non-behavior, resisting the temptation to remark that she didn't either, for the most part, but did not regard this as a special mark of virtue.

"You were in the tub," Jerry said, "and?"

She had heard the telephone ring. She had got out of the tub as quickly as she could, and dried herself briefly, but by then the telephone had quit ringing—

"You didn't know your daughter was in the house?" Pam asked her.

"Why do you say that?" Mrs. Oldham said. "Yes, I knew she was downstairs. Reading, probably. She has to read a great deal for all these courses she's taking."

"Then why—?" Pam began, but stopped, because Jerry was shaking his head at her.

"You got to the phone," Jerry said. "And?"

She had gone to the extension on the second floor, and found that her daughter had already answered. She heard her daughter say, "All right, I'll come over," and then cut the connection.

She had got a robe on, and gone out into the stair hall and called her daughter's name down the stairs and been just too late. The front door was closing, closed. She had gone downstairs, then, hurrying, and opened the door and looked out, and not seen anyone.

"Of course," she said, "I couldn't go out on the sidewalk and really look because I wasn't dressed."

It still, to Jerry, sounded as if Faith Oldham might have been invited to join a friend—for a drink, for a cup of coffee. He said so. He said that, possibly, Faith had thought her mother already asleep and had not wanted to waken her. It was, also, he pointed out, possible that Faith was home by now and wondering where her mother was.

"I wish I could believe that was all it was," Hope Oldham said. "I do wish I could."

Part of it, at any rate, could easily be checked. Jerry asked for a telephone number, got it and dialed it. A telephone rang in the Oldham house. Jerry let it ring for some seconds before he hung up. It didn't, he pointed out, prove anything.

"No," Mrs. Oldham said. "It's no use. She's—she's gone to him. That's the dreadful thing. Deep down, I knew it all the time. He's—he's made her come to him. The poor, poor child!"

Jerry spoke for both of them. Jerry said, "He?"

The expression in the pale blue eyes seemed one of surprise.

"Why," she said, "that Carl Hunter, of course. That dreadful—*evil*—man." She looked from one to the other. "You didn't even suspect," she said, and her tone was incredulous. "He—*took you in, too.*" She shook her head, slowly, as if in despair. "He and the professor," she said. "Two evil men. And evil turned against evil."

The Norths looked at each other and Jerry shrugged. It was Pam who repeated. "Evil?"

"Twisting people's minds," Hope Oldham said. "Making them do—horrible things. Getting *into* their minds, breaking down all the right things—the true things." She paused; she looked at them and shook her head again. "You don't know about such things," she said. "I tried to tell that friend of yours—Weigand?

170

His name's Weigand, isn't it?—what kind of a man Jameson Elwell was. I could tell he didn't understand. Didn't even believe me. And this Hunter—"

She stood up suddenly.

"I've got to go," she said, and her voice now was shrill. "I've got to find her before he makes her be—makes her do some other dreadful thing. I've—"

It was obvious to Pam that hysteria had once again gripped Hope Oldham.

"Wait," Pam said. "There's something you've forgotten. Mr. Hunter—whatever he is, if he's all you say he is—can't do anything to anybody. Not now. He's in the hospital." She paused and repeated the word very slowly. "Hospital. Perhaps you're right. Perhaps Faith has gone to him. But—don't you see?—there are all sorts of people at the hospital. Nurses and doctors and—and all sorts. So—what can he do? Supposing he wants to do anything?"

"They couldn't stop him," Mrs. Oldham said. She spoke quickly, almost feverishly. "Nobody could. Anyway—I called the hospital. He's got around them, too. They said he couldn't be disturbed. She's there with him and—"

She did not finish that. "I've got to go," she said. "Find them."

Jerry said "Wait," this time. He said that, too, was something easy to check on. Probably Hunter was asleep; he might have been given a sedative. It should be easy enough to find out. He looked up the number, he dialed. Answered, he said that he wanted to enquire about a Mr. Carl Hunter. He waited for some time.

"Mr. Hunter," a mechanically pleasant voice told him, "is doing as well as can be expected."

"I wonder," Jerry said, "if I could be connected

with his room? I realize it's late, but it's rather important for me to talk to him. And I understand his injury isn't—"

"One minute, please," the pleasant voice said.

It was a minute—it was more than a minute. And the next voice was not a woman's formally soothing voice. A man spoke. He said, "I understand you want to talk to Mr. Hunter?"

Jerry said he did.

"Who's calling?" the man said, and Jerry told him who was calling.

There was another long pause. It was as if the man had turned away from the telephone, covering the transmitter with his hand. But then he spoke again.

"Sorry," he said. "Mr. Hunter can't be disturbed."

Hung up on, Jerry hung up. He turned and looked at Pam, at Hope Oldham. His face was puzzled, reflecting a puzzled mind.

"They're—" he began, and reconsidered. "It sounds," he said, "rather as if they're keeping something back. Maybe Hunter's worse. Maybe—"

He did not finish. He dialed again. After a little time he was answered by a voice—a somewhat sleepy voice—which he knew well.

"Is he ever?" Dorian Weigand said. "No, Jerry. He was in, too late for dinner. Now he's gone, too early for breakfast."

Bill had gone about ten minutes earlier. She had been in bed, three-fourths asleep; he had been undressing. The telephone had rung. He had said, "Right, I'll be along," and dressed again and leaned over to kiss a sleepy wife.

"Wh—" Dorian had begun but he had said, "Go on

172

to sleep, darling. Tell you all about it in the morning," and then had gone.

"The sort of thing that happens all the time," Dorian Weigand said in the disconsolate tone of one much put upon. "Tell Pam she doesn't know how lucky she is."

Bill Weigand might have gone any place, for any purpose. His sudden return to duty did not, necessarily, have anything whatever to do with Faith or Carl Hunter or, indeed, the Elwell case. But as his wife and the frail, excited woman looked at him, Jerry felt growing uneasiness. They had been very guarded at the hospital; very—careful. Because Hunter wasn't, in fact, there any more? It seemed disturbingly likely.

"I'm afraid—" Jerry began, but Hope Oldham, standing now, her little hands clenched convulsively, interrupted.

"They've let him go!" she said. *"Let him go! To kill somebody else!* Faith. Because she—"

11

News that Mr. Carl Hunter had checked out of Dyckman Hospital, almost as easily as he might have
checked out of a hotel, came roundabout to Captain
William Weigand.

To begin with, it was some time after Hunter had left
that word of it reached a hospital official who realized
that the police might be interested. He had, naturally
enough, called Spring 7-3100, which is the number
listed in the Manhattan Telephone Directory, and had
got a male operator. And the male operator, also
naturally enough, had never heard of Mr. Carl Hunter,
the activities of the Police Department of the City of
New York being many. Several other persons had met
death under suspicious circumstances on that day and
the day before; Professor Jameson Elwell was by no
means unique. There had also been numerous burgla-
ries, a few cases of armed robbery and no end of other
matters.

So there was no reason why the name of Carl

Hunter should at once mean anything to the telephone operator. He did not say "Huh?" precisely, and certainly not "So what?" But it did take some little time for the information to reach precinct, which was interested, verified the fact and, sensibly enough, telephoned Hunter's apartment, where it might be expected he had gone. There was no answer. Homicide, Manhattan West, was next; Weigand came then. A little over an hour had elapsed.

There had been no hold order on Hunter, for reasons which had seemed adequate. For one thing, they had no charge to hold him on, and none in immediate prospect. A police preference that a man remain where he is has no force in law. Hunter was a free agent until somebody said he wasn't, and said why. For another thing, a man shot in the leg at eleven-thirty in the morning does not usually get out of bed at a little before ten at night and walk away. For a third thing, Bill admitted to himself—driving toward Dyckman Hospital at a little after eleven—he had slipped up.

Hunter had been told, first by nurse, then by interne, finally by a resident, that he was being very ill-advised. It would, they told him, do his leg no good. He would, at the least, find movement very uncomfortable. He would probably re-open the wound, which might be a somewhat bloody business.

"Men have walked miles to dressing stations with worse wounds," Hunter said, and signed the releases required, and smiled faintly at dubiously shaken heads. He had, however, accepted the loan of a cane.

"Actually," the resident Weigand talked to said, "he was quite right about men walking farther with worse. As a matter of fact, the wound probably won't open if he's reasonably careful. And this isn't a jail, captain.

175

His signature on the release frees us of any responsibility and—"

Weigand knew. He did not blame anybody. Had Hunter said why he wanted to get up from bed, leaving comfort and medical care, and hobble off into the night?

Nobody could answer until Weigand reached the corridor nurse. She remembered, and Weigand wouldn't believe it. He promised to try. All right, Hunter had said he had to go see about the cats. He said it was his night to see about the cats.

She had supposed, naturally, that he was delirious. But he had no fever and seemed, otherwise, quite composed. He had slept for several hours; the sedation, which had been mild, had worn off. He had said, "Get me my clothes, nurse. Thata girl." It had not been that easy, but it had been easy enough.

And did that about cats mean anything to Captain Weigand? Because she was quite sure that that was what Hunter had said.

It meant something. Briefly, he told her what and her relief was apparent. She was, evidently, a young woman of orderly mind. "Oh," she said, "one of those," and went off to respond to a light which blinked outside a door.

Hunter had not, it was obvious, been abducted. He had, presumably, merely got worried about his cats. Dyckman Hospital is only a few blocks from Dyckman University and Weigand drove there and, after some little search, found a watchman, from him learned that psychological experiments on animals were conducted in Wing A of the Philosophy Building. Weigand crossed the campus, went among dark buildings—but here and there lights burned—and found another watchman, who said he hadn't seen Mr. Hunter, whom he knew, but that Mr. Hunter had a key and was in and out at all hours. "Like the rest of them," the watchman said, rather morosely. If Weigand wanted to show him his shield? Weigand did, and the door was unlocked for him, and he went up two flights and down the first corridor on his right, which ended in a swinging door with glass in it. Dim light came through the glass.

Bill Weigand went into a sizable room which had wire cages down one side. In the center of the room was something which looked a little like a carousel, without wooden animals. There was also a long tube, a foot or so in diameter, with glass windows at intervals in its length. For cats to look out through, presumably.

There were some twenty cages and each held a cat—a black cat here, a red cat here, here a tabby. Bill walked down beside the cages and the cats' eyes glittered at him in the half light. One cat rose up and stretched and another spoke and a third rolled over on his back and held his legs up in the air. They seemed to be contented cats.

Bill walked the length of the room and opened the door of a small office, with desk and typewriter and, on one wall, a chart partially filled with figures. The chart was in columns, with a name at the top of each— Pete, Bill, Betsy, Mehitabel. To each cat his column, Bill assumed. And—dates and hours. He looked. The last entries for this date had been made at 1830. It was to be assumed that, then, the cats had been tucked into bed.

There was nothing to indicate that Carl Hunter had been there. Certainly he was not there now. It seemed that his explanation at the hospital had been disingenuous. Bill was a little disappointed, but not unduly surprised.

It was reasonably clear that Carl Hunter was up to something. It began to appear that the absence of a hold on Carl Hunter had been a more significant oversight than Bill liked to admit. Had he, Bill wondered—going back to his car, driving until he came to an open drugstore, finding a telephone in it—had he been taken in by the apparent candor of intelligent gray eyes, of generally straightforward appearance? Or, perhaps more specifically, by the assumption that a man shot at and wounded during a murder investigation—wounded by a bullet from the gun which previously had killed—is unlikely to be himself the killer?

Of course, Hunter might have something else than flight in mind. He might have remembered something, and gone to check on it. He might have known, in spite of his denials, who had shot him and gone to do something about that. And he might merely have decided to go while the going was good.

In that event, he would hardly get far. They almost never did or, if far, for long. It would be a nuisance, of course. Deputy Chief Inspector O'Malley would bellow. Bill would have to cross that bellow when he came to it.

The telephone in Hunter's apartment, which was not far from the university, was unanswered. Bill considered. He looked up another number, and dialed it, and again a telephone rang unanswered. He let this one ring longer—they might be asleep in the Oldham house. They might be asleep on the second floor and the telephone might ring, dimly, on the ground floor. But, given all reasonable time, nobody answered.

Which was mildly interesting. Faith Oldham and her mother might, of course, have gone downtown to a theater, or to a movie. There is no special reason for two adult women to be home at—he looked at his watch—at eleven-forty. They might be playing bridge, or canasta for that matter, with friends. They might be—anything. It was evident that they were not at home. And Faith and Hunter might be somewhere together. And Hope might be with them? The last seemed a little doubtful.

He rang the Elwell house, and waited, again, for at least sufficient time, and nobody answered there, either. Delbert Higgins, whose presence might be expected, was evidently elsewhere. Or very soundly asleep. Or not wanting to be bothered answering the telephone. Or—anything.

Bill called precinct, which had no word of Hunter. He called his own office, which reported that the Connecticut State Police, asked to go beyond the formality of a report, had admitted not being too convinced, either, that Rosco Finch hadn't been driving a Jaguar in April and wrecked it, and ended three lives. And had pointed out that being unconvinced is nothing to base charges on.

Weigand drove to Hunter's apartment, and climbed three flights of stairs and pushed the bell button. He pushed it for some time, tried the door and then, quite illegally, used a key he was not supposed to possess to unlock the door.

The apartment was small, neat and empty. Hunter had not come home to change his clothes, which one would have expected, since the right trouser leg of the suit he was wearing had a hole in it, and blood on it. Or—if he had, he had not left the damaged suit. Bill

179

could see no reason why he should not have, since the blood on it was his own. There were a good many books in the small apartment, including a good many on hypnotism. There was a typewriter with a sheet of paper in it. There was a single sentence typed on the sheet. "Mehitabel, although evidently superior in Experiment C, failed completely in the two ensuing experiments, conceivably because she does not especially care for liver."

One lived and learned, Bill thought, and continued his quick search. No gun in evidence. Bill had not supposed there would be. A good many manuscripts, presumably also concerned with cats. Perhaps not, of course; it might well be necessary, in time, to read what Carl Hunter had written—on cats and other subjects. It wasn't yet. Bill left things as he had found them, and locked the door, and went down to his car and sat in it.

He sat for a few minutes and rubbed his forehead with the ball of his right thumb. It didn't seem to be coming together—a lot of pieces; no pattern. Finch and the Jaguar, Ames and Faith, Faith and Hunter, Elwell and—Enough for two patterns; perhaps for half a dozen. A policeman's lot is not—

It was as if his mind had fingers and snapped them, quite on its own. It was so sudden, so easy, that Bill considered it with skepticism. But then he said to himself that he'd be damned, and that it was a pattern and perhaps *the* pattern. He talked to his office on the car radio. Mullins was to be rousted out—he was bunked down in the squad dormitory. Or was supposed to be? Was. He was to be told where to meet Weigand. He was to use a patrol car and step on it.

* * *

It took time to quiet Hope Oldham, and at best their success was relative. She became more coherent, but her frail hands did not cease their constant, twisting movement. And there was no stability in her, no real steadying. She would agree with Jerry that they had, really, no assurance that Hunter had left—or escaped from?—the hospital. But, a moment later, she would be shaking again, and saying over and over, "She's gone to him. Gone to him. He'll do what he did before."

And what he had done before was to kill Jameson Elwell. For the money Faith was to inherit from Elwell. Murder Elwell, get the money by marrying Faith, then kill Faith to make the money entirely his. "I know," Hope Oldham said. "I *know!*"

It was not much good to tell her that she couldn't "know." It was not much use to reason with her, although they tried it.

"Listen," Jerry said. "Will you listen? Even if Hunter's what you say he is, if he killed Jamey so Faith would get the money, she's safe as long as she isn't married to him. Don't you see? Her death now wouldn't serve any purpose."

He made it as calm as he could, spoke as if it were obvious. And he was told he didn't understand, that neither of them understood. They didn't understand Hunter any more than they had understood Elwell. They couldn't know what Hunter was capable of. They—

"Wait," Pam North said, taking her turn, trying in her turn to lessen the strange tension which had built up in the pleasant living room, where they had been sitting in such relaxed peace only an hour before. "Wait—you say you didn't know about the inheri-

181

tance. That Faith didn't know. Then how would Mr. Hunter—" Pam caught up with herself, and said, "Oh," before Hope Oldham, in one of her moments of sudden reasonable calm, said that she thought that would be obvious enough for anyone.

"The professor told him," Mrs. Oldham said. "It was all part of—of the plan. You don't understand. The old man—it was enough for him to control people, to twist them. To—have power over them."

Which was, of course, absurd. Pam and Jerry North exchanged a glance, each reassuring the other that this, at any rate, was entirely absurd. Of course, the desire for power, with no other reason than itself, was—Of course it was absurd.

"I suppose," Jerry said, "in Jamey's case at least, you mean—what do you mean? That he hypnotized your daughter? In that way controlled her? But—she told Pam she had never been hypnotized, and Pam was—you were convinced, weren't you?"

"Yes," Pam said. "Only—well, there *is* that other thing. Induced amnesia."

Jerry wished that he had not given Pam the book to read. He somewhat, indeed, wished he had never published Jameson Elwell's book.

"Of course he did," Hope Oldham said. "Now you're beginning—there are evil things, Mrs. North. We try not to believe in them, but there *are* evil things. Things come out of darkness."

It did, Pam thought, seem a little darker than usual in the living room. And of course Mrs. Oldham was only an hysterical woman. Of course there was nothing to any of this. She must keep telling herself.

"Hypnotized her," Mrs. Oldham said. "Made her—feel what he wanted her to feel. Believe what he wanted her to believe. Turned her against Arnold, against me. If she had been herself, do you think—could anybody think—she wouldn't have realized how fine Arnold Ames is? How—how common, how *low* Hunter is? That with Hunter she would be—throwing everything away?"

"You believed this all the time?" Jerry asked. "Were sure this—this influencing of your daughter—was going on? And—all the time that Hunter had killed Jamey?"

She had not said that. She did not pretend that. It was only when she herself heard of the money Elwell had left Faith that she saw the whole thing clearly. "Then," she said, "I knew. It was like a light going on. And now—where *is* she? What is he—"

"Wait," Pam said, "if you feel this way, why don't we call the police? They'll find her—probably they're looking for Mr. Hunter now—and if they know about her—"

And Hope Oldham, her hands twisting again, her voice shrill, said, "No, no, *no!*", each time with greater emphasis, and held her twisting hands up as if to push away some physical threat. Which didn't make any sense at all.

"I don't—" Pam began, but Jerry interrupted. He spoke quietly again, slowly. He said that Mrs. Oldham had forgotten one thing—left one thing out. Hunter himself had been shot; shot from behind, wounded. He could not, from what Jerry knew of it, have shot himself. Of course, he supposed it could be a coincidence but—

"Well," Jerry said, "I don't believe it. I think it was part of—of the rest of it. And that means there was somebody else—somebody else with a gun—and—"

"Don't," Hope Oldham said, and her face contorted. "Don't you see that, either? And you ask why I don't go to the police. How can I?"

Jerry shook his head. But Pam said, her voice steady, but a little higher than it usually was, "You mean you think your daughter shot Mr. Hunter? Carefully, so as not to hurt him badly. So—so that we, and the police too, would think what Jerry just said? That the fact Mr. Hunter was shot at means he wasn't the one who killed Jamey?"

"Why," Hope Oldham said, and was in that instant as calm as either of the Norths—possibly calmer. "Why, of *course*. He hypnotized her and made her do it—gave her the gun to do it with. To clear himself. And *make her guilty too*. Because, it would be a crime to shoot anybody, even a man like that and—it would be, wouldn't it, even if she weren't really responsible? Didn't really know what she was doing?"

Jerry thought a moment. He said he supposed shooting a man, even on his instructions, would still be a criminal action, involving consequences if proved. The circumstances, if they in turn could be proved, would probably extenuate—to some extent.

"And," Mrs. Oldham said, and now there was bitterness in her tone, "you want me to—to help turn my daughter—the poor, helpless child—over to—to that? Call the police in and say, 'Here she is. Do what you want with her'?"

She was dramatic; it was all shrill, overdramatic, as implausible as a dream. It was all—

"Jerry," Pam North said slowly, "it could be the way she says. Couldn't it? Is there any reason it couldn't be? Except—oh, it's bizarre. But—it's possible, isn't it? And—it fits together in a strange, awful way. And—"

She let herself run down. She looked at Jerry and, as she had earlier, Hope Oldham looked at him too, her blue eyes intent. It was as if they both waited a decision, looked to him for it. Which was, Jerry thought briefly, almost the most bizarre thing about this, admittedly, bizarre interlude.

In his mind he put it together, slowly—a need for money, a desire for power; one of two men turning on the other at the end—to hurry the money, perhaps to end the power. They knew only the surface, and that only by hearsay, of the relationship between Jameson Elwell and his protégé, Carl Hunter. Perhaps—There was an infinite range of the perhaps. Hunter, if the "Mr. H." of Elwell's book, as there was no reason to think he was not, was skilled in hypnosis. Faith had turned, apparently very suddenly, from the highly "eligible" Arnold Ames to the notably less "eligible" Hunter. It was quite conceivable that Hunter, if he had wanted evidence favorable to himself—he might have thought the police closer to the truth than, as far as Jerry himself knew, they had been—might have persuaded Faith to wound him slightly. (Trusting optimistically to her marksmanship.) With hypnotic technics or, for that matter, without them. Women in love will sometimes go to considerable lengths. A girl inexperienced, as Faith seemed to be; suggestible, as her mother thought her—well, such a girl might be persuaded to go to quite considerable lengths.

"I suppose," Jerry said, "it could be fitted together this way. I wonder if Bill—"

But there was, aside from Mrs. Oldham's stated

objection, an obstacle to getting in touch with Bill Weigand, and asking him if he had thought of this bizarre theory and, if he hadn't, putting it to him. Bill was off somewhere, probably in search of Hunter. He could, of course, be reached, in time. But if Hunter had the girl, if he was in any way what Hope Oldham thought he was—

"She's all right as long as she's not married to him," Pam said, and Jerry realized that, once again, Pam's thoughts paralleled his. Mrs. Oldham looked at him, her pale eyes very intent. It was almost as if she waited for words sure to come.

"If," Jerry said, "Hunter really has this influence over Miss Oldham he could—take care of that, couldn't he? Simply by taking her to some place—it used to be Maryland, maybe it still is—where there isn't any need to wait to get married. Once they were married—if there was an accident driving home—" He did not finish.

Hope Oldham covered her face with her hands and her body began again to shake. Again Pam went to her. And this time, one of Hope Oldham's thin hands closed on Pam's wrist, closed trustingly. The movement was touching; Pam felt sudden tenderness, a sudden need to protect this tormented woman.

"We just sit here," Hope Oldham said, almost in a whisper. "Just sit here."

There was no reproach in the words, in the tone; there was a kind of resignation in both. But the reproach was, nonetheless, implicit. She had turned to them for help; they were not helping. To hold shaking shoulders, say "there, there" is not helping. Pam turned and looked up to Jerry, looked anxiously.

Anything, or almost anything, would be better than

nothing. Get Bill and tell him; failing Bill, get Mullins. Jerry was at the telephone again, dialing again. "Homicide, Stein speaking." Lucky it was Stein; Stein knew him, time was saved.

Mullins had just left, on instructions from Weigand, presumably to join Weigand. Stein had not himself taken the message. He did not, therefore, know what was up. He would find out. Could he get the captain on the radio? He could try; have the dispatcher try. Have him call Jerry? Right. Meanwhile—

"A girl's—" Jerry began, but Hope Oldham gave a little gasping cry. "Never mind," Jerry said. "I don't think there's anything you can do. Yet, anyway. When we get hold of Bill—"

Stein said, "O.K., Mr. North."

Nevertheless, the police would have to be told. Mrs. Oldham could not protect her daughter from two things at once—from Hunter, from the police. She would have to be brought to see that.

"He can make her say anything," Mrs. Oldham said, still in a low voice, now almost as if talking to herself. "Make her do anything. I know he can—*know* he can. Make her say dreadful things—make up things. We just sit here. We—"

"There," Pam North said, ineffectually. "There. It will work out all right. You're making it worse than—" Than it was? Of course. Hold to that assurance, steady on that. Mrs. Oldham was—what did they say? "Beside herself." Things like this—

"It is comparatively easy for an experienced operator to get a good subject to throw what he believes to be acid toward the face of a person protected by 'invisible' glass. However—"

The sentence popped into Pam's mind. She tried to

eject it. Elwell had said "however." On the other hand—was the pattern of events in which Mrs. Old-ham so apparently believed any stranger, any more difficult to accept than that a man or woman, on instruction, should try to maim, to blind, another, presumably without hatred, without hysteria?

"Nothing he couldn't make her say," Mrs. Oldham said, still as if talking to herself. "Nothing—nothing too wild, too cruel. Nothing—"

"There," Pam said. "There, there, Mrs. Oldham. We'll find her. Nothing will—"

I go on saying meaningless things, Pam thought; go on making meaningless sounds. "There." What does "there" mean? Why say "there, there" when you are trying to soothe, to comfort? Why not—

Pam North stood up very suddenly.

"Over," Pam said. "Not down. *Over.*"

They both looked at her. Jerry ran fingers through his hair, a little convulsively.

"She said, 'I'll come over,' " Pam said. "Wasn't that it, Mrs. Oldham. 'Come *over*'?"

"Yes," Hope Oldham said. "Come over."

"Not down," Pam said. "Don't you see? Doesn't either of you see? If she had been coming here, she'd have said, 'I'll come down.' Because she lives uptown and we here. And if she'd been going to—oh, say the university—she'd have said 'up.' We all do if we live in Manhattan. But—'over.' " She waited.

"I don't know," Jerry said. "East side. West side. Possibly. But—" The "but" was doubtful.

"Or," Pam said, *"to the house next door.* That's what we used to say. Our house was in a row of houses and the girl next door would say 'come on over' and I'd say—Don't you *see?"*

"Well—" Jerry said. "It might be. But—Mrs. Oldham, when she went to the professor's house from your house, didn't she go through the laboratory? And you saw her going out the front door and—"

"Probably," Pam said, "Bill took the key. I'd think he would have. And—Mrs. Oldham, did she have a key to the front door? Of the professor's house?"

"Yes," Hope Oldham said. "And this dreadful man—that would be the place he'd want her to come. It's—it's all arranged there."

She stood up abruptly.

"If Bill took one key," Jerry said, slowly, to Pam, "I imagine he'd take the other. If Faith had both." He paused. "Of course—" he said.

"Hunter would have a key," Pam said. "There were records and things, and if the professor wasn't there and—and nobody was there—"

"That's it," Hope Oldham said. "That's where he's taken her. That—"

She started, abruptly, toward the door.

The Norths consulted, without words. They started after her. Pam paused for a moment; picked up the black purse Mrs. Oldham had left on a table. "You're forgetting," Pam said, and held the purse out to the frail woman. "Or would you rather I carried it?" Pam said, not knowing precisely why she made the offer.

Hope Oldham reached for her purse, the movement automatic, and opened the door before Jerry could reach it and hurried—almost ran—along the corridor toward the elevator. They went after her.

Bill Weigand drove down the sloping block, past the two houses which stood shoulder to shoulder. There were lights visible in neither, which proved nothing.

189

Lights might blaze in rooms at the rear of both, for all one could tell from the street. Bill had to drive almost to the end of the block before he found a place to park the Buick. And, with it parked, he sat in it and waited. He had a wait of about ten minutes. Then a police car, unmarked—at least to public eyes—came down the street. It passed the Buick, moving slowly, looking for a lodging. It reached the end of the block and turned right, and Bill continued to wait.

Sergeant Mullins, in due course, walked up the block and opened the Buick door and got in. He said, gloomily, that somebody ought to do something about the parking problem. "There ought," Mullins said, "to be a law."

"There is," Bill said. "Now—"

He talked briefly. Mullins said "Yeah," twice and "Uh-huh" twice and, "But listen, Loot," once only. Bill finished and Mullins said, "Uh-huh," thoughtfully and then, "It leaves quite a lot out."

"Right," Bill said. "Ever know a time a lot wasn't, sergeant? That half of it gets thrown away?"

"There's that," Mullins agreed. They got out of the car and crossed the street and walked up it to the two Elwell houses. They went down two steps to the entryway of the Oldham house and rang the doorbell. They rang it several times, and waited some minutes, and Mullins said, "Too bad we haven't got a search warrant."

"Very," Bill said, and Mullins took a leather container of keys out of his pocket and tried one of three. "Right on the nose," Mullins said. "Comes from living right." He turned the key and they went into the Oldham house.

190

It was quiet. They listened, not disturbing the quiet.

"Have another try at the bell," Bill told Mullins, and Mullins reached back through the open door and pushed. The bell rang loud in the house. It rang several times.

"We could yell," Mullins said, and closed the door behind them.

"We could," Bill said. "We won't. If there's anybody here, they heard the bell. If they wanted visitors—" He left it unfinished.

There was nobody in the two large rooms on the ground floor; nobody in the kitchen, nobody—dead or alive—in the single bathroom. They went up a flight. The front room—Mrs. Oldham's living room—was empty. So was the bedroom off it—a bedroom with a single window on the street; a narrow room. There was nobody in the bathroom off the corridor which led to the rear of the house; nobody in the two rooms there, the larger obviously Faith's, the smaller apparently a guest room. There were only two closets, one for each of the larger rooms. Mrs. Oldham had a good many dresses in hers; Faith had fewer. Hope Oldham's dresses, Bill thought, were "younger" dresses than her daughter's. There was nobody, dead or alive, in either closet.

"There's the basement," Mullins said. He spoke in a very low voice.

"Go and look," Bill said, and Mullins went downstairs, very quietly, and looked and came back after a few minutes and shook his head.

They climbed the last flight, and Mullins took the key case out. But Bill Weigand patted air with his hand and then put an ear to the heavy door. After a moment, he stepped aside and motioned Mullins, and Mullins put an ear to the door. He stepped back in turn and they moved several steps down the flight.

"Can't get the words," Mullins whispered. "Can you?"

Bill shook his head. They went back to the door. Mullins eased a key into the lock, nodded, and turned gently—very gently, very slowly. There was a tiny metallic sound. They waited. Nothing happened.

Tenderly, by fractions of the inch, Mullins pushed the door open. A crack was enough for the moment.

The voice inside the laboratory of the late Professor Jameson Elwell went softly on.

12

The cab stopped and they went, single-file, Hope Oldham first, between parked cars. Mrs. Oldham was, as she crossed the sidewalk, groping in her big bag. She did not pause, did not wait for Pam and Jerry North. She bent down a little, putting a key in the lock, turning the key. She pushed the door open and they went into the Elwell house and then Hope Oldham called her daughter's name.

And there was no answer. She called again, and no sound but her voice broke the silence in the house. Jerry found a switch; a muted light came on in a ceiling fixture.

"We're—" Hope said, and turned and looked at the Norths, her eyes seeming to pick up the light. "We're too late," she said.

But Jerry shook his head at that.

"If they're here," he said, "if he brought her here as—for the reasons you think—to hypnotize her—to—"

He stopped.

"To what," he said. "What exactly?"

She looked at him, and seemed amazed.

"Why," she said. "Get her to say—make her *think*—that she killed the professor. Get her to confess. I thought—didn't I say that?"

"No," Jerry said. "But—if he's trying that, he'll probably try in this laboratory. Where, as you say, it's all arranged. Set up. And—the lab's soundproofed."

"Yes," Pam said, and now she led—led up the stairs. She went very quickly, very lightly. They followed her, Jerry last.

Pam hesitated momentarily on the second-floor landing, glanced at two closed doors. But then she went on up the next flight. Of course she was right, Jerry thought; if they were to find anything, anyone, it would be in Jameson Elwell's office, or in the laboratory beyond it. He had a stubborn doubt that they would find anything, anybody. The further they went with it, the more improbable it seemed—all of it seemed.

The door to the professor's office was closed. Pam tried it; it was not locked. The door opened inward and opened silently. It also opened on a dark room, and Pam, now, stopped in the doorway. There was a little light, sifting up from he foyer light below.

Jerry hesitated for a moment. Then he reached around Pam, groping for the light switch and found it and again hesitated. Then he pushed the tumbler up. A light went on on the desk—a light in a metal cone. There was no one in the room. But the door to the "closet"—to the passage to the laboratory—was partly open. There was no sound in the room and they heard nothing from the laboratory beyond it. Presumably because the door at the other end of the short corridor, the passage between filing cases, was closed.

Jerry had been in the office only twice—once when he had gone there to talk to Elwell about the book; again when Jamey had given them dinner and, after it, asked if they would like to see where he conducted most of his experiments—his experiments, that was, in hypnotism. "Not cats," he had explained, and Pam had a little lost interest, but gone along all the same.

The door at the rear of the "closet" was, Jerry remembered, a sliding door. So it might be possible—

He went first, now; went between the filing cases in the corridor and reached for the hollowed handhold in the sliding door, and stopped with his fingers in it. Then he put an ear to the door. There was a faint murmur beyond it; the murmur, he thought, of a woman's voice.

He turned back. Mrs. Oldham and Pam stood at the doorway, watching. He beckoned Hope Oldham, used sign language. She put an ear to the door, listened, stepped back. She started to speak, but Jerry tapped his lips with a forefinger, and they went back into the office.

"It's her voice," Hope Oldham said, in a whisper. "I was—we've got to stop it. Before he—"

She did not finish.

"First," Pam said, after it was evident that the older woman was leaving words hanging, "first we ought to find out what—what's really going on. By listening."

She looked at Jerry.

"Without his knowing," Pam explained, to, it occurred to Jerry, the backward.

They could, at any rate, try. Jerry went across the room, flicked off the light. He groped among shadows to the "closet" and into the little corridor and this time they went behind him, Hope first, then Pam. He put fingers back in the handhold and began, gently, to pull the door to the side. "If it makes a noise," Jerry thought, "I've had it—if it makes a noice and Hunter's really this desperate character Hope Oldham thinks he is." Jerry had, then, the unhappy conviction that Hunter probably was just that. What had before—only moments before—seemed entirely improbable seemed now, as the door began slowly to move, altogether too likely. Hunter would hear the door, and Hunter would still have the gun and—

As the crack widened, Jerry moved a little to one side. But then he realized that, by so doing, he put Pam and Mrs. Oldham in the line of prospective fire, and sighed silently, and moved back. Couldn't let the so-and-so shoot Pam.

The door made no sound. When it was open a few inches, and as the murmuring voice became the sound of words, spoken softly, Jerry stopped his pressure on the door. There was space enough to look through, now; they could see, and hear, what they needed to see and hear.

There was a single soft light in the room. It, too, glowed in a metal cone; the cone was pointed toward the wall, reflected from it softly.

Faith Oldham lay on her back on a couch. Hunter sat beside her, faced toward her (so that his back was to the "closet" door, which was a break). He sat with his right leg stiffly out in front of him. (So, he wouldn't move quickly, when he moved; which was another break.)

The tape recorder was on the table beside the couch.

"—of mother," Faith said, in a soft voice, with the intonation of one who ends a sentence. For a moment there was silence. Then Hunter, not much more than a dark shadow against the lighted wall, reached toward the tape recorder. There was a faint click and an almost imperceptible humming began.

"You are Faith Oldham," Hunter said, and spoke very quietly, very slowly and very gently. "You are in an hypnotic trance. You are Faith Oldham, and you are sleeping soundly and you will not waken until I tell you. Then you will waken easily and feel rested and refreshed."

"Yes," Faith said. She did not move, and her eyes were closed. But her voice was quite a normal voice. It was also an oddly contented voice. "I will not waken until you tell me."

"When you do wake up," Hunter said, in the same soothing voice, "you will remember everything that is happening now. You will remember you have been in a trance and what I said and what you said to me. Do you understand that, Faith?"

"I—" the girl said, and then hesitated. "I will remember?"

"Yes," Hunter said. "I am making a recording of what we are both saying. You do not mind if I make a recording?"

"No," Faith said. "That's all right, Carl."

Her tone, the whole grouping of her words, was so natural, so much what one might have expected from a person awake, that Jerry North wondered, fleetingly, whether this was a charade—a charade played for their benefit. Or—and this was more probable—for the benefit of the tape recorder. But then this, he thought, would be a preposterous overproduction. It had been going on before they came; he was almost certain that Hunter did not, now, know that they were there. If a charade for the recorder only, why the couch, the closed eyes? The recorder would not register that the eyes were closed. If for the recorder, why not sit somewhere in comfort—Hunter certainly did not look comfortable—and read lines into it? He groped briefly through his few, and rather dim memories of Elwell's book; came up with something. Good subjects in hypnosis behaved, spoke, so naturally that no one could detect hypnosis.

Jerry's thoughts ran under the words of the two in the laboratory. He heard the words.

"You have been hypnotized before," Carl Hunter said. "You remember that now. Do you remember that?"

"Yes," Faith said. "Now I remember. But—I'm not supposed to remember. When I'm awake I won't remember."

"This time you will remember," Carl Hunter said. "Do you understand me, Faith? When you wake up this time, you will remember all that has happened. You will waken when I tell you to, and you will remember all that has happened. Do you understand me, Faith?"

"I understand."

"Jamey hypnotized you before," Hunter said. "That is right, isn't it? He explained what he wanted to do and you went into a trance—went to sleep. As you are now."

"Yes," she said. "It happened four or five times."

"That was Professor Jameson Elwell? That is the one you mean when you say Uncle Jamey."

"That's a silly thing to say, Carl," the girl said. "Who else would I mean?"

"I know," Carl said.

"And," Faith said, "you asked me all this just now. Just before."

It was obvious enough to Jerry; to the others waiting in the wings. This time it was for the record; this time to make a record to be heard by others. But—Jerry thought—could anything really be done with such a recording? For whatever purpose Hunter wanted to use it? It didn't seem—

"I know," Hunter said. "Jamey hypnotized you several times. He always told you that when you waked up you would not remember. And, that if somebody asked you, you would deny you had ever been hypnotized. Isn't that right, Faith?"

"Yes," she said.

"But now you remember," Hunter said. "You remember all about the other times, don't you?"

"I remember," Faith said.

"He hypnotized you to help you. Isn't that right, Faith?"

"So I could be myself," the girl said. "That's what he told me. When he waked me up, I would be myself. I would not be under—under—"

She hesitated. For the first time there seemed to be a struggle in her mind; conflict in her mind.

"Under the influence of somebody else," Hunter said. "Who, Faith?"

She hesitated.

"Who, Faith?"

"Hope."

Hope Oldham drew in her breath sharply, almost as if she had been struck. She moved. Jerry took her arm, pressed hard, and she looked up at him. There was just enough light for him to see her face; she formed words with her lips, without sound. "I told you," the lips said.

"Who is Hope?"

"Why do you ask that?" the girl said. "You know, Carl."

"Who?"

"My mother."

"Why do you call her Hope?" Hunter said, softly, the voice very soothing.

"She wants me to."

"Why? Do you know why? Did Jamey tell you why?"

"He said I must understand why. That that was part of what I had to do to—to be myself. He said I must decide whether it was to—to tie us more closely together. Not only as mother and daughter—as contemporaries. To draw me back into her life. He said— he said that children and parents break apart as the children grow. He said the way cells divide, and that that is the way things are meant to be, so that each person can be himself. He said that if that seemed right to me, I must—must have the strength to make it right. Whatever appeal she made."

Holding her arm, trying to quiet her, to keep her from the movement that seemed imminent, Jerry could feel Hope Oldham's body move convulsively. He pressed more firmly.

"Go on, Faith," Hunter said. "What else did he tell you about this? And—did he tell you much the same thing each time he hypnotized you? You were willing for him to hypnotize you, weren't you?"

"I was—I felt guilty," Faith said, seeming to answer the last question first. "After—after you and I met.

Because it seemed wrong and she kept saying it was wrong, and that it was my duty to—to her."

"Your duty to do what?"

"To marry Arnold. But after we met—"

She stopped at that. Jerry had, momentarily, a feeling that Hunter had pressed her too far. Sometimes—another dim memory from Elwell's book—didn't the best subjects awaken, unexpectedly, when pressed too far? When the mind encountered a block?

Hope Oldham pulled at Jerry's arm with her free hand, and gestured, and he bent down to her. Her lips were against his ear, he could feel her breath on his ear.

"You see what they did?" she whispered, and even with her lips so close he could just hear her. "What he's doing now? The—poison? We've got to stop—"

Jerry shook his head quickly. He reversed their positions. "Wait," Jerry whispered. "Wait!"

He was not sure she would.

"Let him give himself away," Jerry whispered. If that wouldn't do it, nothing would. She pulled back a little and stared at him in the dim light. He couldn't tell anything from her face.

She should be willing to wait, Jerry thought; should even be eager to wait. Because Hunter was, methodically—and for the record!—proving that what Hope Oldham had charged was true; that Elwell, and now Hunter himself, had worked to influence Faith's young—unsure, too trusting—mind; had sought to come between the girl and her mother.

"What else did he tell you?" Hunter asked. He had been silent for some seconds. Possibly, Jerry thought, to let the block in the girl's mind dissolve. "About you and your mother?"

"That was all," Faith said. "Oh—he said it each time and told me to remember, but not remember I remembered. Once he said that animals were wiser about parents and children. Mother cats, he said, know when it is time for kittens to be on their own, and push them away when it is time. And that if the kittens stay around and grow up, the mother cat just thinks of them as other cats, and lets them be other cats. He said that, of course, that was a good deal to ask of humans."

Again, Hope Oldham snatched in her breath. Jerry could not tell whether in indignation or, as seemed equally possible, satisfaction at a point proved.

"Faith," Hunter said, "did you know that Jamey was sick? That he wasn't going to live more than a few months? Did he tell you that?"

"Yes."

"Was that when you were in a trance?"

"Yes, Carl."

"And told you that you would not remember that, either, after he had waked you up?"

"Yes."

"Did he tell you that he was going to leave you money?"

"Yes, he told me that. He said he knew that we needed money and—and—"

Again it seemed as if her mind were blocked.

"Go on, Faith," Hunter said. "Go on. You are to remember everything, Faith. Everything."

"That if I had money of my own I wouldn't need to feel—responsible. Responsible about that. That it wouldn't need to be part of any decision I made."

"But you were to forget that, too, when you were

awake? That he had said he was going to leave you money in his will?"

"Yes."

"Did he say why he wanted you to forget it?"

"No, Carl. But it wasn't that, especially. I wasn't to remember anything when I waked up. Was to deny that I had ever been hypnotized."

"I know," Hunter said. "Faith, did you ever do anything you couldn't explain to yourself—or to anybody—after Jamey hypnotized you? During the period he was hypnotizing you? How long was that, by the way?"

"About two weeks," she said. "You mean, when I was awake? You mean posthypnotic suggestion, don't you?"

"Yes."

"Once," she said, "I went and looked in an old suitcase. In the storeroom. It was—all at once I had to go look in the suitcase. I had to find something."

"What?"

"I don't know. It was always—shadowy. I felt it was something I had put there, or seen somebody put there, when I was a child. But it never had any shape."

"Did Jamey tell you to look there, do you think?"

"I don't know. I don't think so."

"Did he have you remember things about your childhood?"

"Sometimes. Twice, I think."

"And you remember—half remembered—that there was something in the suitcase? And he planted a posthypnotic suggestion that you go and look?"

"Carl, I don't know. I don't remember."

Now there was evident strain in the girl's young

voice; a kind of lost quality in her low-pitched voice.

"You don't need to remember, dear," Carl Hunter said. "Don't be worried, Faith. You didn't find this—whatever it was?"

"No. There wasn't anything. Wait—there was a collar button. Papa used to wear stiff collars. It was probably one of his."

"But not what you were looking for, was it?"

"No. Of course not."

The strain had gone out of her voice. Again, it was difficult to believe that she was in a trance of any kind, was not as fully awake as Hunter obviously was.

"And that," Hunter said, "was the only thing Jamey ever had you do—directed you to do—when you were awake? The only thing, I mean, that might have grown out of a posthypnotic suggestion?"

"Yes," she said. Then, "I don't remember anything else."

"Faith," Hunter said, and spoke more slowly even than before, "you will remember everything. Everything Jamey told you. Told you you were to do. You cannot help remembering, Faith. When I tell you to remember everything, you must remember everything. You cannot help yourself. Do you understand, Faith?"

"Yes," she said. "I must remember everything. I cannot help remembering."

"And telling me what you remember."

"And telling you what I remember."

Was there, now, a different quality in her voice? As if now she were indeed asleep, and talking in her sleep?

"Did Jamey tell you that he was going to die slowly, and in pain? That the pain had already started?"

For some seconds, Faith did not say anything.

"You must remember," Hunter said, his voice gentle, insistent.

"Perhaps he did," she said, finally, as if the words came with difficulty. "I'm trying to remember, Carl. Perhaps he said something like that."

"I'm not trying to put anything in your mind," Hunter said. "Only to get you to remember. You know that, Faith."

"I know that."

"Did he say anything about euthanasia? That those hopelessly ill should be let die? Even helped die?"

"I don't remember that."

"He believed that, Faith. He told me he believed that. He never told you?"

She stirred for the first time; stirred restlessly on the couch.

"You are deeply asleep," Hunter said. "Deep, deep asleep. You will not waken until I tell you to. You are deep, deep asleep. You will not waken until I tell you to."

He paused a moment.

"He never told you that, Faith?"

She was quiet now.

"I don't remember that," she said.

"Or—asked you to help him?"

She moved her head a little from side to side. She said, "I don't understand what you mean."

"Help him die," Hunter said. "That it would be the act of a friend to help him. That there would be no guilt in helping him, but only a generous action. That he would see no harm came to you. Would arrange that you would not even remember what you did. Would see that nobody else ever knew what you had done."

"Don't, Carl," the girl said. "Don't, Carl."

"You must remember everything," Carl Hunter said.

"I can't," she said. "I can't remember that, Carl. I can't remember anything like that." She was quiet for a moment. "I couldn't hurt Uncle Jamey," she said, "I couldn't have hurt Jamey."

Again she moved restlessly on the couch.

"Faith," Hunter said, "did your father ever have a gun? A revolver? When you were a little girl did you know your father had a revolver?"

"I don—" Faith Oldham said. "No—wait a minute. There was—something. Something shiny."

"Think of it," Hunter said. "Think of it and you will remember it, Faith. It is a long way back but you will remember it. What was the shiny thing, Faith?"

She was silent now for longer than she had been at any time before. Hunter waited, any Jerry and Pam and Hope Oldham waited. Hope was breathing more quickly; probably, Jerry thought, they all were. He turned enough to see Pam, standing on the other side of Hope Oldham and a little behind her. Pam's face was tense.

"It was a revolver," Faith said. "I remember it. The barrel was what was shiny."

"You saw it? Your father had it?"

"Yes. Yes. That was it."

"Faith. Did Jamey ask you about a revolver? Your father's revolver?"

"No. I'm sure he didn't."

"He told you—instructed you—to go the storeroom and look for something in a suitcase? Under posthypnotic suggestion?"

"Yes. It must have been that."

"And—bring him what you found there?"

"I don't remember that. But there wasn't anything in the suitcase—"

She stopped. Again she stirred restlessly.

"But he put it there," she said. "I remember seeing him put it there."

"Who, Faith? Jamey? Put what? Was it in the suit—"

"Not Uncle Jamey," the girl said. "I told you that. My father had the revolver. He put it in the suitcase. It was a long time ago when I was a little girl and I wasn't supposed to see him, but I did. I was wearing a pink dress and I'd gone to show papa the dress and he was—was putting the shiny thing in a suitcase."

"Yes, Faith. And you're sure—you're very sure—that when you went to look in the suitcase—when was that, Faith?"

"Monday," she said. "I think it was Monday."

"And there was nothing in the suitcase? Except a collar button?"

"Nothing. I know there was nothing."

"There wasn't a gun there? You didn't take the gun out of the suitcase and—"

And Hope Oldham wrenched free from Jerry's restraining hand. She moved very quickly, snatched at the sliding door, grabbed it open. Wood cracked against wood as the jamb stopped it. Jerry reached for her. His fingers touched the smooth leather of the handbag under her arm, slipped from it. Hope Oldham went, half running, into the darkened room and went toward Hunter and the girl, and called her daughter's name.

"*Faith!*" she called, her voice high, shrill. "*Faith! Wake up! Wake up!*"

Hunter turned and began to get up from the chair as the door slammed open. He got halfway up and his injured leg gave under him and he lost balance. He was on his sound knee, clutching the chair, trying to rise.

"Faith!" Hope Oldham said again, and now her voice was almost a scream. "Wake up. *Wake up!*"

The girl lay motionless on the couch, her eyes closed. It was as if she lay, untouchable, in a sheath of glass.

Hope Oldham turned on Hunter, then, and Hunter quit trying to get up and stayed, awkwardly, as he was.

"Wake her up," Mrs. Oldham said, her voice still shrill. "Wake her up. I know what you're trying to do. *Wake her!*"

There was threat in the voice.

The Norths were in the room; in the room, standing side by side.

"Jerry," Pam said. "Her *purse! It's too heavy!*"

Jerry started toward Hope Oldham. Her back was to him; she looked down at Hunter, who looked up at her, an odd expression on his face.

"Wake her up," Hope said again, and this time her voice was quieter. But at the same time, almost the same time, as if Pam's voice had only just reached her, she turned toward the Norths. And then, very quickly, she had the big black handbag open.

She plunged her right hand into the open bag. The hand came out with something shiny in it; with a revolver in it. She stepped back, then, so that she could face both the Norths and Hunter.

Faith Oldham did not move on the couch.

"Don't interfere," Hope Oldham said. And then, to Hunter, "I told you to wake her up. You've done all you're going to do to her."

"Have I?" Hunter said, and his voice was curiously calm. For an instant, Pam North thought that he looked beyond Hope Oldham, standing above him—beyond her and the revolver with a shiny barrel. But there was nothing beyond her, at the angle from which he looked. "What have I done, Mrs. Oldham?"

"We all heard," she said. "I tell you to wake her up."

The gun leveled on the half-kneeling man.

"What?" he said. "What have I been trying to do, Mrs. Oldham?"

"We heard," she said. "I tell you—we heard. And—it's all there, isn't it?" For an instant the gun pointed at the tape recorder. Jerry felt his body twitch forward. The gun swung a little. Jerry stopped.

"If you heard—" Hunter began, but Hope Oldham did not wait.

"Making her believe she killed him," Hope Oldham said. "We heard you—twisting her mind. Making her say—what you wanted her to say. Take the blame for what you did."

"*I* did?"

Hunter's voice still was calm.

"Killed him," Hope Oldham said. "Because you knew he was leaving her money and—you thought you could get it. And—"

She broke off.

"It's all there," she said, and again meant the recorder, but this time the revolver did not point. "And—we heard you. Mr. and Mrs. North and I—we heard you. So you can't—"

Pam North sensed, as much as saw, that Hunter's muscles were tightening, that he shifted his weight slowly, just perceptibly, so that his body balanced on his sound leg. His hands tightened on the chair he clutched. Pam moved, and the revolver swung toward her. There was a kind of frenzy in Hope Oldham's face.

"I said not to interfere," Mrs. Oldham said. "What do you want to interfere for? Wake her up, Mr. Hunter. You've done everything you could. And— *failed*. So wake her up. *Wake her up!"*

Then Hunter started to come up from his crouch and, at that instant, more light went on—the room seemed to glare with light from an overheard fixture.

"Don't try it, Hunter," Bill Weigand said from the laboratory door, and they turned to look at him—at Weigand and, behind him, Sergeant Mullins. Bill had his gun out.

"Don't try it," he repeated. "Put the gun away, Mrs. Oldham. You won't need—"

She seemed, for the moment, dazed. She did not lower the gun. She backed away, instead—backed toward the wall. It was as if she had not heard Bill Weigand. The gun was leveled still.

She doesn't understand, Pam thought. He didn't tell her.

"Mrs. Oldham," Pam said. "It's all right, now. They're the police. *It's all right*. They'll—"

She was looking at Hope Oldham, began to move toward her. But then, from the side—not quite seen; seen as shadow—there was movement. In what seemed the same instant, Jerry was past her; Jerry's hand came down, a fist, on the shining barrel of the revolver.

The revolver went out of Hope Oldham's hand. It made a soft plunking sound on the carpet.

"Why—" Pam North said, but at the same time Bill Weigand said, "Nice going," and Mullins, moving from behind him—moving faster than so big a man had a right to move—was behind Hope Oldham, his hands closed on her arms.

She began to writhe against the hands. She seemed to be trying to reach down, reach to the gun.

"It's no use, Mrs. Oldham," Bill Weigand said, and Hunter got awkwardly to his feet and stood looking at them.

It was as if Weigand had thrown cold water in Hope Oldham's face. She stopped struggling.

"No use?" she repeated. "What do you mean? He was trying to—"

"I heard," Bill Weigand said. "It's no use."

"I don't—" Hope began, but then seemed to crumple in Mullins's hands.

"Right," Bill said. "You do. You're under arrest, Mrs. Oldham. It was a pretty good try. But—" He shrugged. "Homicide," he said. "Also assault with a deadly weapon. But—murder will do."

She did not say anything. She slumped, and Mullins held her up. Weigand moved his head and Mullins said, "O.K., Loot," and took Mrs. Hope Oldham out through the door he and Bill had come in by—come through after some time of waiting, of listening.

"Saw us, didn't you?" Bill said, and stooped down and picked up the revolver—a .32 calibre from which, it undoubtedly would be found, at least two shots had been fired. "Didn't you, Mr. Hunter?"

"Toward the end," Carl Hunter said. "Welcome sight."

He turned away then and looked at Faith Oldham,

who still had not moved; who still seemed sheathed in glass. He turned back, momentarily, toward Bill Weigand.

"I would," Bill said. "She'll have to know sometime."

Carl Hunter leaned down over the sleeping girl; he leaned clumsily, but touched her shoulders lightly, with tenderness, it seemed with tenderness.

"You can wake up now, Faith," Carl Hunter said. "You can wake up, dear. And—you'll remember. You'll have to remember, Faith."

13

Hope Oldham had, Bill Weigand said, turned out to be the confessing type, which was always a convenience. She would probably, of course, turn out also to be the disavowing type. As time went on, he supposed, there would be much talk of enforced sleeplessness, of glaring lights, of food and drink denied, of the mind beaten down until what lips said—and hands signed— was meaningless, must be ignored. She might even bring in the use of rubber hose and other torments. She would certainly allege promises made by the police, deals arranged with the district attorney.

"All," Bill Weigand said, "according to Hoyle."

He was in the Norths' apartment, with a drink in his hand, and it was Friday evening, at the time for drinks. There was a fire in the fireplace, although it had turned very little cooler. And Martini was sitting on the lap of Sergeant Aloysius Mullins, which was not at all according to Hoyle.

"She really doesn't do it to annoy," Pam had explained, when Martini spoke once, in question and, not being answered, went the long way round to the chosen lap. (She went to a chair, to another chair, to a table, to lap. Only she knew why.)

"It's all right, Mrs. North," Mullins said, if with no perceptible enthusiasm. He sat very still. He sipped his old-fashioned warily.

"It's really," Pam said, "because you don't make advances. So many people keep saying 'Nice kitty' and things like that and reaching down to have their fingers smelled. Cats hate anything fulsome, you know."

"It's all right, Mrs. North," Mullins said, and sat very quietly.

"Go to sleep, Martini," Pam said. "You are falling asleep—deep, deep sleep. You can't keep your eyes open." Teeney looked at Pam with interest, from very blue blue eyes. "Shut your eyes," Pam said. "You are going deep, deep asleep. You are shutting your eyes and you can't open them. You are falling into a deep sleep." She spoke soothingly. And Martini closed her blue eyes. It was very gratifying.

"I must admit," Pam said then, "that she fooled me. At the end, anyway. Although I knew her handbag was too heavy. Except that I didn't know, if you know what I mean."

"You couldn't be clearer," Jerry told her, and saw glasses empty, and went to the bar. "Go on, Bill."

It had, Bill told them, been a little odd. Not unprecedented—most confessions included a good deal of self-exoneration. He had never, however, heard a confession to murder which contained, in a curious fashion, so much asservation of superior virtue. It was rather as if Mrs. Oldham, telling how she had killed Professor Elwell, and tried to kill Carl Hunter, expected it all to end with a rising vote of thanks, tendered her for duty faithfully performed.

"In short," Bill said, "it was Elwell's fault entirely. And Hunter's fault. Both were—are—evil men. She kept using that term—'evil men.' And she was mother defending young."

"To put it in the vernacular," Jerry said, distributing drinks, "she's nuts."

Possibly, Bill said, that would serve—would very roughly serve. Not, however, in a court of law. At least, he assumed it wouldn't. The point had not been raised, of course, before the magistrate, who had remanded Mrs. Oldham without bail, pending a hearing a week hence, which would never be held because a grand jury would intervene with an indictment, charging murder one.

Insanity would be offered at the trial, Bill supposed. He did not see what else could be tried, since Mrs. Oldham had, among other things, been caught with the weapon on her. But that was not primarily his concern.

"Of course," Bill said, "she might get a jury with a prejudice against hypnotism—a feeling that it's a kind of black magic, a kind of witchcraft. And that its practitioners are—witches, I suppose."

"Wizards in this case, I'd think," Pam said.

Wizards, magicians, voodoo doctors. Anyone who seemed to bring up the dark things, the horrid mysteries which are buried only consciousness-deep in the human mind. "A New York City jury?" Pam said, doubt in her tone. She was told that juries, anywhere, can be a little odd, and said she supposed so.

"It was because Elwell was doing—doing things to Faith's mind?" Pam said. "Perverting her mind? Turning her into a zombie? But—he wasn't. She's a perfectly sane young woman and now she's out from under mama's thumb—''

That was, summarized—very much summarized—the burden of Hope Oldham's confession, which was at the same time an assertion of her innocence. Men like Elwell, debauchers of youth (of the mind of youth; she did not go farther) should be destroyed. And Hunter was as bad. They had only to remember what they had seen—this to Weigand, to Mullins. They had seen Hunter at it; seen how he had tried to make an innocent child believe herself guilty.

"But," Pam said, "he didn't. It's—confused. She admits she did it—killed Jamey. But she says at the same time that Hunter was trying to make Faith believe—'' Pam shook her head. Moving it, she noticed that she was being regarded by Martini, who had both eyes open. "You are falling deeply asleep," Pam said, in automatic parenthesis. "Deep, deep asleep. You will not wake up until I tell you to. She can't have it both ways."

"She's not an especially logical woman," Weigand said. "At best. Now she isn't at her best, of course. She didn't seem to realize that the two things cancel out—that one cancels the other out."

"While we're on that," Pam said, "what *was* Hunter up to? Just finding out that Faith remembered her father had had a gun? That the gun had disappeared?"

It had not been that, Bill said. At least at first; at least according to Carl Hunter. Who had, incidentally, got briefly back to his cats, but was spending most of his time holding Faith Oldham's hand, figuratively and, it was to be supposed, literally.

"It needs it, the poor child," Pam said. "But—what was it really? Not just because she thought Elwell was a—a wizard. Somebody from the lower depths."

"My dear child," Jerry said, in a tone meant to annoy. *"You!"* Pam said, but waited. "She had always dominated the girl," Jerry said. "That was important to her. The most important thing in her life because, among other things, it was a way of staying young. By not being relegated, losing out. And also the deep satisfaction of having power."

Pam looked at him skeptically, and also with enquiry.

"Not I." Jerry said, quickly. "I speak in the abstract."

"You'd better," Pam told him. And looked at Bill Weigand.

"We could," Bill said, and smiled at both of them over a cocktail glass, "keep it simple. As it will be kept for a jury. I don't deny either of these—what? Freudian?—theories. An emotional woman's fear of what she did not understand. An aging woman's desire to dominate—to keep power over youth. But—simply—a greedy woman's desire for money. Of which, remember, she hasn't much. And it's been clear all along she hated not having much."

"But," Pam said, doubtfully, "you mean she *did* know about the money Jamey was leaving Faith. I thought Mullins was sure—oh."

"Yes," Bill said. "Not that money. I don't think she knew about that. I'm quite sure—Hunter's quite sure—Faith didn't know about the inheritance *when she was awake*. That Elwell had induced amnesia. The money—the entirely new way of life—they would both have had if Faith married Arnold Ames. Or

217

somebody like Ames. That was the simple motive."

And—they had heard, from Faith, that part of Elwell's effort to free the girl from her mother's dominance had involved encouraging her to live in her own way, follow her own feelings. Which would not, it was clear, lead her to Ames.

"You mean he really—broke that up?" Pam asked this. And Bill Weigand shrugged, and looked at his empty glass, and at his host, who rose in hostly fashion.

They would, Bill supposed, never know about that. It was not a thing on which a finger could be precisely put. Ames had already, perhaps, turned wary, partly because Mrs. Oldham seemed in rather hot pursuit. At least, Ames himself implied that. Which might be a salve to his own pride. But it did seem very probable that Elwell had done at least part of what Mrs. Oldham thought he had, and done it intentionally.

"Playing God," Jerry said.

"For good purpose," Pam said. "Anybody looking at her and Hunter can see that." But, if not Ames, perhaps somebody else, equally desirable? But not if Hunter got too far. She tried to blame it on him?

She had certainly known he was at the house at approximately the right time. Sitting in her chair at the window, she had seen him leave. If the police decided he was the killer, it would amount to a bonus.

"Two wizards with one stone," Pam said, and there was a momentary pause.

Mrs. Oldham, once her daughter had left Wednesday afternoon, had gone through the laboratory to Elwell's office, and shot him, and returned the same way. And then gone out herself and—

"Wait," Jerry said, "she *did* have a key to the

laboratory then? You mean, Jamey had given her one, too?"

Not intentionally. He had supplied Faith with a key to be copied after she had lost hers—two keys, as it turned out, one being to the front door of his own house. But it was Mrs. Oldham who took the keys to a hardware store and had duplicates made. "Enough," Bill said, "to go around. She was the one who did the errands. She made a great point of that."

Hope had thought that, with Elwell dead, she would have no difficulty in reassuming dominance over Faith, redirecting her toward a profitable marriage. But, with Elwell dead, Faith had turned not to her mother but, more fully even than before, to Hunter. And the police did not seem to accept Hunter as the killer. "She blamed us for that," Weigand said. "Pointed out that if we'd been up to the mark we'd have seen he was the obvious one. If she'd succeeded in eliminating Hunter, it would have been our fault for not having him safe in jail."

"Hunter knew she was the one who shot him? That was what put him on the right track? And then—that was why he hypnotized Faith. To find out about the gun and—"

But Pam stopped, although she had been reasonably triumphant. Bill was shaking his head.

"At one stage," Bill Weigand said, "you had the theory that Faith might have killed Elwell. Under hypnotic suggestion. As an act of mercy. Well—Hunter got the same theory, decided to hypnotize Faith and find out. So he would know what he had to protect her from. He says, 'So I could help her if she needed help.' It was when he convinced himself she didn't that he started to make the recording, and to search around in her mind—that's the way he phrased it, incidentally—to find out what he could. And stumbled—he says it was a stumble—on the gun."

There was a considerable silence, then. Bill finished his new drink. He said, "Well—"

"Wait," Pam said. "Mrs. Oldham came to us—got us to go with her—why?"

She had, Bill said, been afraid that Hunter would get to Faith, would hypnotize her. Mrs. Oldham had gone to the Norths to light a back fire, plant a theory. The theory: that Hunter, himself the murderer, would try through hypnosis to make Faith believe herself guilty, bring her to confess guilt. So—

"Actually," Pam North said, "all the time all the poor thing had to do was wait a few months. And Jamey would have died and Faith got the money and—nobody would have had to kill anybody."

She put it succinctly, Bill agreed, and stood up. Martini, seeing movement, jumped from Mullins's lap. Pam looked at her reproachfully; said she was a bad subject, that she was supposed to be asleep.

"Come on, sergeant," Bill Weigand said. "These people—"

He stopped and looked intently at Sergeant Mullins, who had not responded. They all looked at Mullins. *"Sergeant!"* Bill Weigand said, with more emphasis. And Sergeant Aloysius Mullins slept. Then Jerry and Bill looked at Pamela North, whose eyes rounded.

"Goodness," Pam said. "I—*I really did it*. But I must have hit the wrong one. Goodness! I—I was aiming at Martini and—"

They waited.

"Sergeant," Pam said, her voice very clear and decided. "Sergeant Mullins. You can wake up, now."

There was a moment of some tension.

Sergeant Mullins opened his eyes.

"Did the Loot-I-mean-captain tell you that this Old-ham dame admits cooling the professor?" Sergeant Mullins asked.

Home delivery from Pocket Books

Here's your opportunity to have fabulous bestsellers delivered right to you. Our free catalog is filled to the brim with the newest titles plus the finest in mysteries, science fiction, westerns, cookbooks, romances, biographies, health, psychology, humor—every subject under the sun. Order this today and a world of pleasure will arrive at your door.

POCKET BOOKS, Department ORD
1230 Avenue of the Americas, New York, N.Y. 10020